TARA AND EVAN

THE 1800S EXPERIMENT

SARAH LAMB

CONTENTS

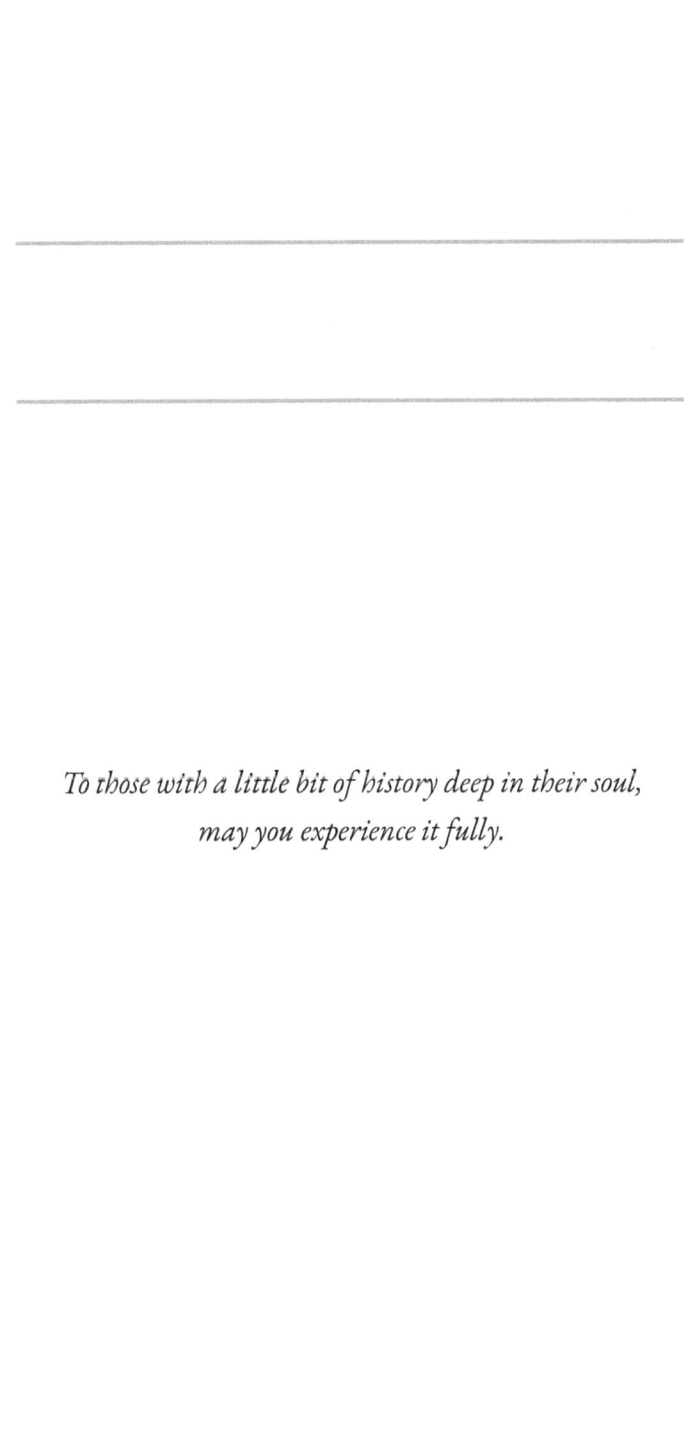

To those with a little bit of history deep in their soul,
may you experience it fully.

CHAPTER 1

Tara James scanned the seemingly endless emails in her inbox. One of these days she'd do a massive deep clean out. She was sure she didn't even remember signing up for half of the junky newsletters in there. Why didn't she ever get anything good?

In between the usual mass of offers to buy a car warranty or claim her inheritance as the only relative from a prince in some non-existent country, something caught her eye. She blinked a few times, but it still read the same—*Finalist for 1800s Survival Challenge!*

"What? No way," she muttered, and clicked on the email. It seemed to take forever to load. "Come on, hurry up," she said to her ancient computer.

One day while at the mall, there had been someone passing out audition applications for a new reality TV series. Lured by the premise, she and Evan, her almost boyfriend, had signed up for it. It wasn't just the form they'd filled out, but each had given a quick on camera interview.

The show was seeing if modern day people could survive a month living like they were in the 1800s. No internet, no phones, no electricity, no indoor plumbing. Honestly, it didn't sound too bad to Tara. Well, except for the indoor plumbing. She enjoyed that perk of this time period. The rest, she was sure she could handle easily. Books, movies, it didn't matter, she loved it. The slower time, the people who seemed to enjoy each moment, felt content at the end of the day, built lasting relationships with those around them...it would be kind of fun to live like that.

Holding her breath, she read the email carefully, then read it again. It looked pretty legit. Was it? There was only one way to know. Grabbing her phone, she sent a text to Evan. Had he gotten one too?

Hey, just got an email. Remember that show we signed up for? They picked me!

She didn't have to wait long before her phone pinged.

Same! Think we might win? Will we get to work together?

Don't know. Would be fun!

It would also be a little tricky to take that much time off of work, so Tara figured she'd best go check in with her boss now. Evan was likely doing the same. She scooped up the files that she needed to drop off anyway, and headed over to Lindsay's office.

Lindsay Madison, her best friend since middle school, was also her boss. Well, second in command of the place but still her boss. After college, where she had studied fashion design, Tara had applied for an intern position with Lindsay's mom's company: Madison Apparel. They designed medical uniforms. Not exactly the high fashion she'd hoped for as a teen, but she really enjoyed it, and in two short years had worked herself up in the company.

Now, at twenty-four, she was in charge of selecting the fabric from suppliers and helping redesign their entire line this year. It was a big deal. And one that she relished being part of.

But sometimes...no, if she was being honest with herself, a lot of times, it felt like something was missing. She was getting tired of trying to figure out what it was. Maybe the chance to live simply, to think and focus on her life, would help her narrow in on it.

Every day had felt like the same since the newness of the job wore off. There were endless emails, a frantic pace to keep up with, clients to make happy, suppliers to keep on schedule, designs to sketch out to encourage people to buy their new apparel right now, and from them.

Tara passed a cluster of interns arguing over a design they'd been asked to create. They looked upset and frustrated and she completely understood. Tara shook her head. *Glad that's not me anymore.*

When she first started working there, she wondered, how much pizazz can you really put into scrubs, or how different could you make them to convince people that they had to have the newest designs in your catalog?

It was surprisingly stressful, and even though it was her job, a small part of her also didn't like the idea of telling people to buy new things all the time, acting like the new version was so much better when it really wasn't.

At a meeting this morning, she wanted to ask why it was so important to encourage slate-gray uniforms to replace the steel-gray ones that a major company had bought last year, but she held her tongue. After all, this was what paid the bills. There was just an uncomfortable feeling inside of her though, and she didn't like it.

Was it really that she didn't like to sell to people? That she simply wanted to design? Or was it something else? That feeling of not being content with her life had been happening more and more. She couldn't help but wonder if there was something better, more fulfilling, waiting for her.

Tara stopped outside of Lindsay's open door and tapped. Her friend looked up, the phone in her hand, and waved her in. "I don't care what you need to do to make it happen," she said to whoever it was on the phone. "Those catalogs need to be shipped by the end of the week and our website updated. Call me tomorrow with a status report."

Lindsay hung up, and smiled at her friend. "Thanks," she said, as Tara set down the files.

"No problem," Tara answered, then took a moment to enjoy the view. Lindsay had a small office, but it was a corner one. Though only a few stories high, from her windows the bustling city beckoned, with perfectly manicured lawns and trees along with flowers in their beds.

"It's beautiful, isn't it?" Lindsay said, nodding at the park. "They just planted the pink flowers over there, whatever they are."

"It is. But it's almost too perfect." Tara crinkled her nose as she eyed the landscape critically. It really was. Flowers were planted in perfect rows, the trees were all trimmed to the same shape, and everything looked as though it had been done in some precise way designed by someone with an architectural degree. Even the park benches each sat in the same direction.

Lindsay laughed. "That is so you," she exclaimed.

"Can I help it if I prefer natural landscapes?" Tara shrugged. "There's just something amazing about nature's own beauty. It doesn't have anyone telling it what to do or how to be, restraining a tree and making it only grow in one direction, even if it was meant to be in another. Have you ever seen a field full of wild flowers? Or tall grasses waving in the breeze? It's breathtaking."

Lindsay shook her head. "Now you just sound weird. What have you been reading? Another historical fiction? Can you imagine what those people had to go through way back when in the olden days? Books and movies make that stuff sound better than it is, you know. Those people all had to pee in the woods. Or in a pot they emptied."

"Yeah, I know," Tara said. "But there was good stuff too."

"Like what?" Lindsay asked. She shook her head. "No way, we've made progress. You couldn't pay me to live back then, even if some of those actors in Regency movies are swoony."

Tara knew that her friend didn't fully share the same tastes as she did in books or movies. In her leisure time, she enjoyed watching TV shows like *Little House on the Prairie* and *Dr. Quinn Medicine Woman*. She also enjoyed reading novels that were set in that time period. In the summer, she had a garden and was teaching herself to crochet. So what? Everyone had something they enjoyed. That didn't make her weird, even if others might think those were old-fashioned hobbies.

"It was a lot of work back then," she agreed finally, "but there always seemed to be such a happiness and satisfaction at the end of the day."

"Don't you feel that now?" Lindsay asked, raising her eyebrows. "You work just as hard as anyone here. Maybe even harder at times. Did you not just sell thirty thousand uniforms to one of the largest hospital systems in the East?"

"I guess," Tara said reluctantly. "But something just feels different as of late. It's like I'm wondering if I'm doing the right thing with my life. I mean, today I had to spend nearly an hour convincing someone that the uniforms they bought a few months ago weren't nearly as good as the almost identical ones we are offering this year. It's...I don't want to say soul sucking, but it's...I don't know. I don't feel as happy as I used to."

Tara stopped the sigh she was feeling. Lindsay didn't understand. This was her life. She'd grown up with this, and the puzzled look on her face said she didn't understand why Tara didn't enjoy what she was doing. Tara decided to press ahead. "Anyway, that's kind of what I wanted to talk with you about."

"Oh?" Lindsay asked. "What's up?" She sat behind her desk, reached for her coffee mug and took a sip.

Tara took the chair across from her, and squeezed her hands together, suddenly nervous. "I need a favor. It's about Evan, too."

"Don't tell me you guys are getting more serious? It's about time!"

Tara couldn't help but laugh at her friend's hopeful expression. She wanted Evan to be more serious too. They'd been friends forever, and somewhere along the way she started to fall for him. Some days she thought he felt the same, others she couldn't tell.

"Well, no, it's not that exactly," Tara said. She swallowed and felt her heart hammering. What she wanted to ask was for the time off to be on the reality television show and to spend an entire glorious month with Evan, doing something she'd always dreamed of. But how could she do that? Reality sunk in and her shoulders slumped. What company would just let someone leave for a month? Was she going to have to give her notice?

It was a really tough choice thinking about choosing between something that sounded incredible and amazing while being with Evan, and staying, working at the job she had put so much effort into that paid her bills and put a roof over her head.

Tara took a moment to try and organize her thoughts and then glanced up at Lindsay who was staring at her with a look of concern.

"If something's wrong, you can tell me," Lindsay said.

Tara bit her lip. "It's just I have a really big favor to ask and I don't want to put you on the spot because you're both my best friend and my boss and I don't want there to be some sort of weird conflict of interest thing that makes you uncomfortable."

Lindsay smiled broadly at her. "And that's why you're not only my best friend but a fantastic employee," she said. Her voice softened then, "But I'm not going to know what it is you want to ask me unless you tell me. So just say it. I'm not going to get mad at you."

Tara nodded. "Okay, a while back Evan and I were hanging out at the mall. These people were doing auditions for a reality television show, and we thought why not?"

"Oh, I think you mentioned something about that," Lindsay said. Her eyes got big. "Wait a minute! Don't tell me! Did you guys get chosen to be on it?" She leaned forward in excitement. "What's the prize? Is it like a million dollars or something you have to fight your way through a jungle to get? Your own private island you could win? Or a house in the Caribbean filled with cute singles you get to date?"

Tara laughed while she shook her head. She was glad her friend was so excited for her. "No, it's none of those things," she said. "But it is something pretty exciting to me. We did get chosen and the filming lasts for about a month. It takes place in Pennsylvania and the four of us would be living as though we were in the 1800s. But then that leads to the problem of my needing to take off of work."

Lindsay leaned back and gave a slow nod. "Say no more. I understand," she said and opened her laptop and started tapping on the keys. Tara wasn't sure what she was doing and she didn't want to ask. Lindsay was a lot of great things, but she was also kind of irritated when someone interrupted her when she was thinking.

About a minute later, Lindsay looked up at her again, her expression serious. "Okay," she said. "What are the dates?"

Tara pulled up the email on her phone and skimmed through until she found it. "The morning of July eighth is when I'm supposed to get there for outfitting and rules. We start filming that afternoon. We'll be filmed for four weeks, then on the twenty-ninth day, they tell us if we won."

With a quick nod, Lindsay turned her laptop around and sat next to Tara on the opposite side of the desk in the other vacant chair. "You have two and a half weeks of paid vacation time," she said, pointing at the screen. "I'm willing to authorize one additional week of unpaid vacation time as a one-time performance bonus for the sales you made. That just leaves the problem of three days we need to figure out. I have to be fair to the others."

Tara squeezed her best friend's hand. "Does that mean I can go?" she asked.

"Well, it means you're going to have to figure out a way to get approval for those three days, or else come back early if they don't let you go late. I can't really give you any more unaccounted for time, even if I really wanted to. There is a company to run and you have a large role in it."

"I understand," Tara said, biting her lip in thought. "There's got to be a way."

Lindsay tapped a perfectly manicured fingernail on her laptop. "Let's keep thinking," she said. They were both silent for a moment, then Lindsay said, "I don't want to suggest lying, but do you have any sick days saved up?" she asked, resuming her tapping on the computer.

"I do, Tara said. "Six days because I've not had to use them this last year."

"Perfect. That's your three days then," Lindsay said, satisfaction in her tone, "because mental health falls under a sick day request and I really can't think of anything more mentally healing for you than getting back to nature and living in your own little prairie house for a month. Once you get there, have to pee in the woods or a smelly little outhouse covered in spiders, you'll see how great it is here, and come rushing back with open arms."

Tara squealed, "You are the best friend and the best boss ever!"

Lindsey rolled her eyes and said, "Just don't let that get around. I don't want people thinking that I was playing favorites."

"I definitely won't," Tara assured her.

"Message me while you are gone," Lindsay said. "I want to know how it's going."

"If I can I will, but I assume they're not going to let us have any electronics or any communication devices except for in an emergency." Tara gave an apologetic shrug.

"Oh yeah, that's right," Lindsay said. "You'll be living in the stone age. I don't know...you're a better woman than me. I couldn't go a day without internet, let alone a month."

Tara rolled her eyes. "You've just never tried. I like unplugging on the weekend. I wish I could do it for more than a few hours, but there's always a work emergency. I really am excited. Even if I do have to use an outhouse."

"It sounds like a dream come true for you," Lindsay said. Then, she searched her friend's face. "Just promise me you're not going to have so much fun that you won't want to come back."

"No chance of that," Tara said. "I love working here with you."

"Even though you called it soul sucking?" Lindsay asked, one eyebrow arched.

"Yeah," Tara said. "But I'm hoping to come back with a huge cash prize, having had a relaxing vacation, and maybe use the time to think about my future and what I want out of it."

"And maybe get a serious boyfriend?" Lindsay teased.

Tara didn't answer, she just grinned as she waved and left her friend's office. She did have to get back. As she made her way back to her own desk, a little niggle of a worry wrapped itself in her mind. Sometimes hardships drove people apart, and living like in the 1800s was sure to have a few difficulties.

This really might be the perfect time to get closer to Evan without any distractions. They'd been friends a really long time and she wanted more. But would he be willing to take the next step in their relationship? Or was this going to be an on camera disaster waiting to happen?

CHAPTER 2

Evan Adams grinned as he watched Tara walk into the room. They hadn't been allowed to see each other until each of the show's contestants had left the "old world behind" as the producer had said, and had changed for their new adventure.

Admittedly, he felt a little awkward in the clothes he was wearing, a green checkered shirt, incredibly stiff pants with a pair of suspenders that dug into his shoulders, boots a little too tight, and a hat he'd sat next to him. The clothes were okay, he guessed, but he sure wasn't a hat person.

Part of him still didn't know why he was there. It was true, Tara was the idea person and he often just went along with it. She had the best ideas. Seemed to know what she wanted in life. Him on the other hand? He'd always struggled and never quite found the right fit for him. It was just easier going along with what others wanted.

Not that she'd have said anything if he wanted to do something different. To be honest, being on this reality show sounded pretty fun. He couldn't wait.

Tara looked around the room, and her face lit up as she caught sight of him. He loved when she smiled like that. It made his pulse speed up every time—especially when that look was directed toward him.

She rushed over and they gave each other a tight hug. "I cannot believe we are here," she said.

Evan couldn't help but laugh. Tara was practically squealing. She hadn't been joking about her enthusiasm for the role when they'd auditioned. Right now, she even looked the part of someone from the 1800s. She was wearing a light blue dress with tiny flowers that nearly came down to her ankles, as well as some sensible boots covered in buttons and her hair pulled back into a braid that had been twisted into a bun.

He didn't know a lot about women's fashions back then, but he thought all she really needed was a bonnet and she'd fit right into the time they were supposed to be living in. Tara looked completely comfortable and at ease. But then, it didn't matter what she wore. She was always like that. Tara was comfortable in her skin completely, no matter what.

That was one thing Evan had always liked about Tara. She also didn't try to be something she wasn't. Authentic was the word that came to mind when he thought about her. She always smiled, had a good attitude no matter what was going on, and got so enthusiastic at times when she was talking, it was fun to get swept away with her.

A twinge of envy ran through him. Tara also seemed to have it all together. She always had, it seemed. They'd been friends since they were in middle school, and he couldn't ever remember her struggling with fitting in. When they moved into high school, then college, she knew right away what job she wanted and seemed content there.

A far cry from him. Too many long days doing the data analysis for the company, and little else, was grating on him. A change would be nice. Would be incredible. But what? He'd spent so much on his degree, and all the other jobs available were doing something similar. He wasn't wanting to leave his company, where he'd built up so much time off and great benefits, just to start over again doing the exact same job, this time at the bottom rung.

He was stuck there. There was nothing left for him but to make do. He'd spent years doing just that. It never felt easier, but what else was there for him? Maybe, at least if he was in a relationship with Tara, he wouldn't have to make do. For once, he could feel solid, like things were going right. The thought made him feel a little better. He was going to do it. He was going to ask her to be his girlfriend. Make it official. Consider a future together.

Yeah. It was a good idea. So was being on the show. Maybe this was just what he needed. Something different to help him refocus on himself and his career, his future as a whole, and figure out what he was looking for. Or at least how to find some level of contentment.

A month without deadlines, frantic bosses, and enough time to relax with his favorite person in the world sounded pretty good to him.

Tara stepped back from the embrace, and Evan didn't have time to do more than pull himself from his thoughts and say hello because the producer clapped his hands loudly and they quickly grabbed seats in the large room.

The producer, a guy in his thirties dressed in a polo shirt and jeans, gave a wave and said, "Okay, now that we're all here let's make introductions. Hi everyone, thanks for coming. My name is Jeff, and I'm in charge."

He pointed to a few other people in the room who were leaning up against the wall. "Let me start off by saying these are our historian helpers. They have made lists for you guys to help you stay in character while on the show. For example, the list will have your chores that you'll need to do daily and weekly as well as instructions on how to do them if you aren't already familiar with how things were done in the 1800s."

Jeff paused and then grinned, "Because let's be honest, I don't know the last time any of us used a washboard to wash our laundry or had to start a fire and cook over top of the stove in a cast iron pan you can barely lift. It's better you have at least a little bit of a heads up on how long that process might take so you don't starve while you're there for the next month."

Tara clapped her hands together and giggled. Evan looked across at the other guy who was grinning at her and the other girl who had a wary look on her face. It was pretty obvious that Tara was the most excited of them all. He sure hoped some of that enthusiasm rubbed off on him.

Truth be told, if it wasn't for Tara, he wouldn't even be here. Living without the essentials in life, like internet, take out, and television was going to be hard.

"All right, so the way it's going to work," the producer continued, "is we have cameras set up in every room and every building except for the outhouse. Rules are pretty simple; you're going to live like you're in 1890. No modern conveniences other than those that were considered new at the time. You've got to follow the rules of the time period. Basically, you'll be acting as though this is your home. You'll tend to the animals, the garden, and improve the area by working on building a barn. And if you can stick it out the whole month, no going against the rules, getting all your chores done and not quitting because it's too hard, then you'll each win $100,000."

Jeff paused then, grinned at them, and added, "Now, it gets even better. If you can stick it out the entire month, in addition to the cash, you have the opportunity to win a huge prize."

"What is that?" the other guy asked. Evan wondered when he'd find out the guy's name. No one had made introductions yet.

"Can't tell you that," the producer answered. "I'm still working on the details but it's something pretty big."

"What if someone doesn't do their fair share?" the other girl, the one with dark hair asked.

The producer nodded. "Great question. Well, that means the contestant doesn't get their portion of the prize money, even if they stick it out the whole month."

"And if they quit?" Evan asked.

He didn't miss Tara's panicked look. "I'm just asking," he assured her.

"If they quit, same thing. No prize. Don't know why anyone would want to quit. I mean, it's all expenses paid, chance to earn more in a month than most people make in a year, and the chance for the killer prize." The producer grinned. "But anyway, if they do, I've got a list a mile long of backup contestants willing to step in, and take a prorated prize amount."

The contestants nodded, and Evan found himself looking again at Tara. He reached over and squeezed her hand. An entire month with all expenses paid and the opportunity to spend every minute with the girl he had been emailing and texting and phoning constantly for years? All that time to work up the nerve to go a step further? He couldn't think of anything better, honestly.

"This is going to be great," he leaned over and whispered to her.

"We are totally going to make it through. A month will be so easy," she said, pretending to flick dust off her shoulders.

"Right. Easy money," he agreed.

"I know it," she said, almost squealing. She turned to him with her big smile and rested her head on his shoulder, when the producer stepped close, resting a hand on his a rm.

"That's another thing," Jeff said as he looked at them. "I know that you two are a couple. However, you're not married and in 1890, unmarried couples did not stay in the same house. In fact, they weren't usually alone with each other either."

"Oh! We aren't a couple," Tara said. "Just...friends."

While she stammered, Evan couldn't stop the look of horror that he was sure was on his face. Not be alone with Tara for the entire month? How was he supposed to make their relationship more formal if he couldn't even spend time with her? He had no idea this was going to happen. Suddenly he was starting to have second thoughts about this whole experience.

CHAPTER 3

Tara looked up at the water dripping from the wood ceiling of the small cabin she was staying in. Of course it would have to be dripping right over top the pot of stew she was trying to stir for dinner that night. Hopefully, it wouldn't be adding any sort of a weird flavor. Or something that would make them sick.

She was trying as hard as she could to keep up with proper hygiene and keep the food area sanitary, but it sure wasn't easy, living like this. There wasn't proper soap, getting hot water was difficult, and there seemed to be more dirt than not. *No wonder in the 1800s many people didn't live past their forties.*

She took a long, slow breath and closed her eyes. It was only the second day, and already she was starting to have her doubts about this entire month-long adventure.

It didn't help that she felt like she was doing almost all of the "female" chores on her own.

At first, it had all started off exciting enough. Tara and Evan had met with another couple, Mark and Jill, who were joining in this month-long challenge to see if they could live as though they were in the 1890s.

The producer had explained everything from the beginning so that everyone knew what to expect, and had one last chance to back out—not that she was going to. He had explained that there were to be no modern conveniences. If they needed water, it had to come from the well and be drawn up with a bucket.

He did assure them that the water had been tested to be sure it was safe, and as long as they only took water from the well to drink they wouldn't get sick. Also, there were no washing machines, refrigerators, or electric cook stoves. There was no electricity, so at night they would have to use lanterns and be very careful not to burn down the houses.

None of that had fazed Tara at all. She was feeling incredibly confident as he spoke and was thinking that the month was going to fly by. That is, until they were told the living arrangements.

It's not that she was planning to share the same room with Evan, but they weren't even in the same house. Because none of the couples were married, they put Tara and Jill inside of the two-room house with a loft, and put

Evan and Mark inside of another, smaller building that was a single room.

Immediately, Tara was a little disappointed. This had been her chance to try and spend a lot of time with Evan. Her daydreams of cozy evenings by a fireplace as they talked about their future fizzled, just like the fire in the stove kept doing because of the damp firewood. But of course, she should have expected that, and remembered that in the 1800s, everything was a lot more restricted compared to today. It wasn't just by social or economic class, but also by gender roles.

Tara and Jill had a massive list of jobs they were expected to do every day. The guys had one too, though that didn't stop Jill from moaning and complaining all the time about the girl's list. Tara hoped she'd survive being trapped with her. Already Jill was hardly doing anything to help. It was pretty obvious she didn't want to be there, which made Tara wonder why the other girl had even agreed to come.

Jill could have left. In fact, at any point, any of them could leave. That was a promise made by the producer. If someone did leave, that meant they'd give up any chance at the prize. Jill had said several times she wasn't there for the money. So, Tara wondered, if she hated it so much, why was she still here?

Tara covered the stew and listened to the hiss of steam as the occasional raindrop from the ceiling fell onto the hot lid. Maybe one of the guys could get up on the roof tomorrow and patch it. She sure hoped so.

Tara carefully took a rag and used it to open the door on the stove and pushed in a stick of wood, then brushed her hands off on her apron. She wasn't completely sure if the cast iron stove was the right year, but didn't plan to say anything. It was nice to have a flat top to cook on. At first, she'd been worried she'd have to cook over a fire, and wasn't looking forward to the smoky smell all the time, or the smoke filling the house. Thankfully, this stove was here and was doing a pretty good job.

Jill was scowling in her seat at the table, slowly snapping green beans that they'd picked fresh from the vines before the rain had moved in. The girls were responsible for things like the meals and caring for the smaller animals like the chickens. They were also responsible for the large garden that had been planted a couple months prior so that it would actually be giving them produce while they were there.

Fighting the weeds in the garden was going to be quite a task, Tara could see that. However, there really wasn't much time, as important as the garden was, to work in it. Everything had to be done efficiently and quickly, because there was so much to do.

The girls also had to keep the stove going and keep the house clean, which was a lot harder than it looked on TV with a dirt floor and walls made with chinking in between the wooden boards.

The chinking was really mud that sometimes flaked off, so that just as soon as you finished sweeping the floor you turned back around and there was some more to sweep up. Thankfully, they all agreed to try and do as much as they could to take care of themselves, like each person doing their own laundry and picking up after themselves. That would help a little with the workload.

Despite Jill's grumbles, the guys didn't have it that easy either. They had horses and cows to take care of alongside pigs. That meant cleaning the stable, feeding and watering the animals, and tromping through muck. They were also given the job of sawing trees and making boards out of them, so that if all went well the settlers, as they called themselves, could build a small building to be used for supplies and their food stores for the winter.

And speaking of small outbuildings? That's exactly where they had to go when someone needed to use the bathroom. Tara was beyond grateful that it was new and didn't stink much, but she was sure as the time went on it would be absolutely horrible and disgusting. She was dreading trying to wash her hair tonight. Evan had suggested they take turns bathing in the nearby creek, but she and Jill had opted for the large tub, and slowly heating water up.

What she wouldn't give right now for a proper shower, with hot water that flowed from the tap when she turned it on. Still, she refused to let herself get discouraged. They'd hardly been there. Of course everything was different and felt hard right now. She wasn't used to it. In a week, she'd be a pro.

The thought made her smile, and she hummed quietly while she resumed stirring the stew. It really looked quite tasty, and she was curious to try it.

Jill pushed the bowl of beans away from her at the table. "How is it you're always so cheerful?"

Tara shrugged. "Just how I am, I guess," she laughed. "I've watched a lot of historical shows and love reading books about this time period, so I knew what to expect with some of these things." She stirred the pot again as the rain beat against the roof. "That said, I'm honestly kind of irritated with the rain right now. I don't like the drippy roof and that means tomorrow it will be extra muddy outside. And I'm also a little bit irritated that we don't get to spend more time with the guys. I really thought there would be more opportunities to do that. I also didn't think I'd be so tired. Or be so hot standing over the stove cooking."

She tugged on her long-sleeved dress. She had pushed up the sleeves, but it hadn't helped much. Without air conditioning anywhere, she felt sticky, and the steam from the stove didn't help. An icy drink and fresh clothes that didn't cover her from throat to ankle would be so nice. But that wasn't happening anytime soon. Both were off limits.

"I don't know what I was thinking, agreeing to this." Jill sighed, and laid her head on her arm.

There was a soft plop, and Tara looked at the ground. A small notebook had fallen onto the floor. Jill pounced on it, and Tara pretended not to see it. She'd seen Jill with it a few times, each time all sneakily. At first, she wondered if it was a journal, they were allowed to do that, but now she wasn't too sure. She typically was muttering or had a look of pure concentration on her face when she was writing frantically in it.

Jill shot a worried glance at her, but Tara kept up her pretense, as though she'd not seen anything fall. Instead, she picked up the list of things they were supposed to do tomorrow. "Maybe when the weather is nicer you will feel better."

"I doubt it," said Jill. "Tomorrow we're all supposed to go foraging in the forest for mushrooms and berries. Do you know how soggy it's going to be? All the mud to get out of our clothes. The bugs. Uggghhh. I hate nature. There are so many bugs."

"If it keeps raining like this," Tara consulted the long list they were given, "we are supposed to card wool and make yarn."

Jill groaned. "I don't know how in the world we're going to do this. The wool is greasy, and it smells funny. It's also dirty. There's little bits of stuff in there I don't even want to think about what it might be."

"It can't be too hard," Tara said, though admittedly, Jill was starting to fill her mind with doubts. Jill was also right about the wool. There was a large pile of it to wash, removing the dirt, bugs, and other soil she didn't want to think about.

At another groan from Jill, she bit her lip and tried to sound positive. "I'm sure we'll figure it out. I saw it done once at a living history museum. It seemed easy enough."

Jill didn't answer, she just let out another sigh, and started complaining about all they had to do. Pressing her lips together and ignoring her, Tara went to the front door and opened it, peeking outside. About a hundred feet away, Evan stood at his door too. They smiled at each other, but then he went back inside.

Tara tried not to feel a flash of hurt. She knew it was raining, and the rules said they couldn't be alone together, but surely the guys could have come over and visited. They hadn't all day. She was sure they'd show up for lunch, but wasn't sure how long they'd stay. Was this all harder than Evan had expected? Was he feeling a little resentful of her for dragging him into it?

There was another loud groan, followed by a wail that would have been enough to try anyone's patience. Tara closed her eyes briefly. If only she could be with Evan right now instead of Jill it would definitely be a lot more enjoyable.

CHAPTER 4

Evan sighed and rolled over, trying to get comfortable. It didn't matter which way he turned. The lumpy straw pallet was not an inviting bed. He knew the girls had the same setup, though they did have low frames for their beds.

So much for the relaxing time he thought he'd have. Evan snorted. At first, he had thought he'd just wake up, go through the day relaxed. He'd do the chores, they wouldn't be that hard, right? Afternoons would be relaxing. Maybe fishing, or reading. Evenings would be spent playing board games or cards or more reading. He'd spend time with Tara. Everything would be movie-like. Nothing stressful. Nothing hard.

This was the total opposite. They had more animals here than he'd thought there would be. There were temperamental cows, chickens who liked to attack you, horses who pooped way more than he thought possible, a garden that didn't stop growing weeds, and of course, a huge list of jobs that needed to be done in order to fully get the whole 1800s experience. There was more, but he was too tired to think about it. That was another thing. This manual labor was wiping him out.

Even the lure of the huge cash prize had dimmed. Though he wouldn't mind a hundred grand sitting in his bank—or a portion of it after he had a little spending fun—there were moments he'd give it up just like that. For example, this morning, when the cow had backed into him, sending him slipping in the pile of...well, he didn't want to relive that. But he sorely missed being able to get into a shower. They each had three sets of clothes. Three. And he wasn't sure he'd ever get that stink out of that one, even though he had it soaking in a pail.

Honestly, if he didn't like Tara, and wasn't trying to do this mostly for her, he'd have seriously considered going home by now.

Except...except there was something about this place that just felt...he wasn't sure. There was plenty of time to figure it out though.

Sighing, Evan rolled over again.

"Can you quiet down and get to sleep?" Mark grunted. "Morning comes too quick here. There are pigs to feed, cows and horses to take care of, and those blasted trees to saw. Man, I can't wait to get back to civilization."

"Sorry," Evan said. "Just trying to get comfortable."

"I gave up on that a week ago," Mark grumbled.

"Has it already been a week?" Evan asked. He thought for a moment and then counted. Yep, it sure had. "The days are blending together," he said.

"And one seems like four, with the amount of work we have to do," Mark added. "My blisters have blisters, and we've hardly completed anything on that list they gave us to do. Some settlers we are."

Though their small room was dark, Evan could hear Mark twisting around on his pallet, trying to get comfortable as well. "Maybe it will get easier," he suggested, though it was a halfhearted comment. If anything, the last week had been torture in many ways.

First, it had rained for four days straight. Everything was musty smelling and mucky to walk through. Everyone was tired and crabby. Even Tara had lost some of her cheerfulness at the situation. To top it all off, he hadn't even gotten to spend even a few minutes alone with her. Someone always seemed to show up, or they remembered the cameras pointing at them.

With those cameras, they couldn't do much at all. He knew they weren't allowed to stay in the same house, but what about hand holding? Talking quietly? A walk alone? It was driving him crazy trying to find out. He'd decided that he wanted to talk to her, take things to a more serious place. At first, Evan had thought this would be the perfect setting, especially with how crazy Tara was over this time period. Now, he wasn't so sure. If anything, living like this was creating one huge barrier and a lot of tension. And not the good kind.

There had been a few moments alone, but Tara had put distance between them. When he said something, she shrugged, and had said she was trying to follow the rules. While he hadn't let on, that had upset him a little. Surely they could at least sit closely. Did she really have to be such a stickler? *I mean, sure, it would be nice to win a hundred grand each, but they wouldn't disqualify us, just for a little hanging out. Would they?*

It also was pretty tough not to have the things he was used to and had always taken advantage of, like hot water when he wanted to shower, a TV to veg out in front of. Hot crispy French fries, gooey pizza, and—his stomach growled in longing and Evan rubbed it.

Yeah. There was a lot he missed. He was willing to give it up for Tara, and a chance at a hundred grand. He just hoped he made it that long.

A rhythmic breathing from Mark alerted him that his new acquaintance was asleep. Evan wished he could get his mind to settle. So far, nothing had been like he'd thought. Originally, he'd pictured himself and Tara, well, almost living like they were in a TV show. They'd cook together, laugh together, do chores together…they'd get to spend time looking at the moon and the stars, maybe laying on a pile of soft hay. Who knew hay would be so scratchy? He sure hadn't, until he'd stop to rest and thought the pile looked inviting. He'd itched for hours afterward. Never a gain.

Though he was worried about how things seemed to be going in the direction he didn't want with Tara, undeniably, there was something enjoyable about being here. He was learning new things, doing daily activities differently from how he'd ever done them, and, interestingly enough, at times enjoying it.

Take the food, for example. After a long, hard day of chores, a simple meal of stew and biscuits tasted better than his favorite burger joint back home. Couldn't replace the French fries and pizza though. He couldn't wait for those. Evan thought about asking Tara and Jill if they could try and make them, but Jill would likely say something like how those didn't exist in the 1800s. That girl sure did like to rile him up. He wasn't sure why.

Evan opened his mouth to ask Mark if he felt the same, but a soft snore reminded him that Mark was asleep. Evan stared into the darkness and tried counting. One, two, three... He got in the three hundreds before he finally fell asleep, and it felt like he'd only just shut his eyes when the sun shone right into them. The front door was open, and Mark was at it, whispering to someone. Jill? Why was she there? He sat up and pushed off the blanket.

Mark turned and shut the door. "Morning, sleeping beauty," he laughed.

"Ugghhh. Morning came too soon," Evan yawned. "I see the sun is out."

"Yep, and just in time for chores," Mark said.

There was a knock on their door, and Mark opened it to find Tara standing on the other side. "Breakfast is ready," she said, "whenever you are."

"Be right over," Evan said, alert now as he sat up. He hurried to wash his face in the washbasin, smooth out his hair, and grabbed his last clean shirt and pants.

As they were about to leave, Evan saw a small book on the table. "Where did this come from?" he asked, flipping it open.

It was filled with rules and advice about everything 1800s. His eyes landed on a line about something called courting, which a quick skimming of the text showed was sounding a lot like dating. He'd have to read more of this later.

"Oh, I found it yesterday," Mark said. "Thought it might be interesting to read."

"Yeah, looks it," Evan agreed. He looked down again at the page.

"We better hurry," Mark said. "The girls are waiting."

"Yeah, right," Evan said, and they went outside. "Laundry day for me this afternoon," he said as they walked over to the house the girls were in.

There was a large table with four chairs sitting outside, and the girls had platters loaded with breakfast. It looked like eggs, sausage, oatmeal, and bread with butter and jam this morning.

Mark offered, "You do mine, and I'll take care of all the animals."

"I'll do it all," Tara offered, overhearing them. "I don't mind. I've actually gotten the hang of it."

"She has," Jill agreed. "Tara is way faster than me, which is why I'm making lunch today. She's doing the clothes washing."

"Do you mind?" Evan asked. "Some of it's pretty muddy from all the rain."

"Not at all," Tara said. "If this was really back then, that's what the women would do."

"I'll grab it after breakfast," Evan said.

"In trade, you have to haul the water for me," Tara said. "We have to heat it up in the big pot in the yard." She pointed to a tripod set up with a large cast iron cauldron. "I need that one full so I can heat it, and then I need that large bucket filled too, for rinsing," she said and pointed to a huge pail.

"No problem," Evan said. "Mark and I will help." Truthfully, he hated hauling water. It seemed inefficient, but there wasn't any other choice.

"Thank you," Tara said. "It takes a lot of trips."

Her grateful smile made him feel better.

"I wonder how long it took before indoor plumbing was common," Jill said. "At least for water. The sheets are going to be hard enough for you to wash today. I can't even imagine the blankets."

"I wonder how often they even washed them," Tara said, her nose crinkling a little.

Her expression was so cute, Evan fought the urge to lean over and kiss her nose.

"Here," Jill said, setting down four mugs. "There's coffee and tea. Or I guess you can go milk a cow."

Everyone laughed at that. "I guess that's what they did," Mark agreed. He helped himself to the butter. "Is there more?" he asked.

"Butter?" Tara asked. "We need to churn it. I'm going to work on that this afternoon."

Evan cleared his throat. "I was also hoping you'd go for a walk with me this afternoon."

She smiled at him. "I'd love to."

"You can't go far," Jill reminded her. "We have to stay in sight of the cameras."

"Oh yeah. I actually forgot about those," Tara said.

"Good thing I reminded you then," Jill smirked. "Wouldn't want you two to be embarrassed on TV when this airs." She made kissing sounds and Mark snorted with laughter. "Or kicked off the show," she added.

Tara rolled her eyes, but Evan saw her blushing. "Whatever," she said, looking down at her plate.

They finished the last few bites and Tara gathered the dishes. She placed them in the bucket and poured the steaming kettle over them.

"I'll grab the laundry," Mark said, and left. Evan nodded and glanced over at Jill, who had gone into the house. He stood, and through the window saw her on a bed, hunched over.

"She do that a lot?" he asked Tara, jerking his thumb at the door.

"You mean, skip out on all the work?" Tara asked. "Yep. All the time. I'm sick of it, but there's nothing I can do. I hope when they edit the show, they'll show that part."

"Probably not, with the way those people do stuff," he said, and started drying the dishes, then stacking them on the table.

"You might be right," Tara agreed. She bit her lip as though she wanted to say something, but her face changed, as though she thought better of it.

"What are you thinking?" Evan asked.

She faced him, her hands still plunged into the water. "Do you think there's something weird about her?"

"Weird? How so?" Evan glanced back at the house.

"I mean, she doesn't help much, she disappears for long periods of time, and she's got this little notebook I see her writing in pretty often. Whenever I get close, she stops writing and glares at me."

"Why do you think that is?" Evan asked.

"I don't know. Which is why I was asking you if you'd noticed anything weird about her. Or Mark."

"I can't say that I have," Evan said, frowning. "But I'll sure be watching now." He picked up the dishes and headed toward the house. He stopped suddenly. Through the window, he could see Jill hunched over still, but this new angle let him see a small notebook in her lap and a pencil frantically scribbling.

When he'd stepped close to the house, he must have made a sound, because she quickly thrust it under her pillow, and pretended to be straightening the blanket. Evan didn't say anything as he walked the dishes to their shelf, and then out again.

What was Jill up to? He had a feeling it wasn't anything good. And now, he was curious about Mark. Was he up to something too? He'd seen the two of them whispering a few times. In fact...more than a few times. Like this morning. And they always seemed to stop when he got close. It was getting weird.

At first, he thought they were just flirting. But now he wondered if it was something a little more suspicious. Were they out to sabotage him and Tara in some way? What would even be the point of that? Evan crossed his arms and scanned the area slowly. Jill and Mark were at a corner of the house whispering again.

Yep. They were definitely up to something, and he was going to find out what it was.

CHAPTER 5

Tara straightened and rested a hand on her aching back. It hurt almost as much as her hands did. Laundry by hand, and for four people no less, was really hard. Evan had also brought her a bucket with a filthy shirt and pants and, red-faced, apologized that he hadn't been able to get the smell out, and wondered if she could help.

Geez she really missed automatic washing machines and detergent, microwaves, dishwashers, and other modern conveniences.

TV shows and movies seemed to gloss over the dirty parts of pioneer living. As hard as she thought, she never recalled Caroline Ingalls or Dr. Quinn looking hot and sweaty and exhausted while doing chores. That slightly irritated her. This physical labor was so much harder than she realized it would be.

Sighing, Tara tried to reframe her thinking, like the book on how to be happy at your workplace she'd been reading before she came out here suggested. She didn't have to be here. She got to be here. There was a difference, and really, this was a great opportunity. She was just tired and hot. That's why she was cranky.

And as much as she wanted to go for a walk with Evan later, it might be all she could do just to stay awake while sitting. She was so tired. And hot. And thirsty. What she wouldn't give right now for a cold glass of soda. The bubbles fizzing. Tiny pops of moisture brushing against her nose as she leaned in. Mmmm. The smell of—

"Tara!" Jill called. "Just hang the rest up after lunch. It's ready."

Shooting a quick look at the laundry basket and then the sky, Tara nodded. The clothes could wait for a half hour, and would still dry. The sun wasn't going anywhere today. Sitting down for a little sounded really nice.

Years ago, she'd read a fascinating article on the washing machine. Historians had talked about how the automatic wringer was life changing for the women. She'd believe it. It was ridiculously hard to wring out the clothes. Her hands ached, and the sheets...she was just going to hope they dripped dry. How in the world would she ever wash the heavier blankets if something happened to them? She might not even be able to lift them when wet.

Wearily, she went over to the table and dropped herself before the bread, salted meat, cheese, apples, and butter and jam Jill had sat out. Seeing the small portion of butter nearly made her groan. She'd almost forgotten they had to churn more butter this afternoon. It was an important part of the diet. With all of the physical labor done each day, having fat in the diet was critical, they'd been told.

However, it was one of the most difficult things to do. She and Jill had churned butter when it had been raining, but that was exhausting work. Her arms still ached from it. The plus side was that she sure wouldn't have to worry about exercising while out here—all the chores worked her body like never before. Every inch of her seemed to ache at night. Maybe that is why the women wore dresses all the time. No waistband for if they went up or down in size. The idea wasn't a bad one.

One thing for sure was the next time she went to a grocery store, she'd be grateful to buy butter, not make it, even if the freshly made did taste fantastic.

Mark plopped down across from her. He looked irritated. "You okay?" she asked as the others joined them.

"It's that cow," he said, spooning strawberry jam on a slice of bread. "The big one."

"What about her?" Evan asked.

"She keeps hitting me with her tail when I milk. I even tried to lean in close like to avoid her. You know, like they told us too. I swear, it's like a whip when she hits me. She finds me no matter what position I'm in and beats the heck out of me while I milk. My face still stings."

"At least she doesn't kick over the pail," Evan said. "That would be worse. No milk or butter, and we need both."

"Not you she's beating up," Mark grumbled. "You do it tonight, see how it feels. At least she didn't push me over today. Sorry about the laundry, Tara."

"Maybe she's flirting," Jill laughed.

They all laughed at that, and then louder at the story Jill told about her first attempt at flirting in middle school, when she kept swinging her ponytail around and ended up getting it caught on an earring.

Under the table, Evan's slightly rough hand brushed against hers, and Tara squeezed it in return, hoping no one saw. She was worried about Jill and her notebook. Was she trying to get dirt on her and Evan to knock them out of the show?

She glanced down. They were sitting next to each other, with a proper distance between them, but it still wasn't close enough for her liking. Judging by how often Evan reached across her or toward her, he felt the same. Her heart sped up a little. Did this mean Evan was finally interested in taking things a little more serious?

Their nearness, and his actions, made her glow inside. Yes, they might be forced to keep a distance between them, but she now understood the appeal. There was an anticipation for each next moment they could spend together. At least, on her end. She had no idea how Evan was feeling. She could only hope.

Even though they'd known each other since they were teenagers, Tara felt like she didn't always know what he was thinking or feeling. It frustrated her sometimes. Evan didn't ever usually say what he wanted to do or how he felt about something, just went along with everyone else. That was all well and good, but she always worried that he might get resentful at some point.

Just then, he smiled at her, and Tara shivered. Yes, it was obvious he was feeling something too. What was going to happen at the end of the month? She was hoping they'd be even closer than before. Much closer.

"If someone eats the last piece of bread, I don't have to put it away," Jill said.

Tara shook her head. Mark grabbed it, tore it in two, and handed half to Evan. "Thanks for lunch," Mark said.

Feeling a little better after a break, Tara rose. "I've got to get the rest of that laundry hung up," she said. "Can you get the cleanup, Jill?" At the other's nod, she left the table and headed back to the laundry basket.

Tara spread the first piece of laundry out on the line, then looked up as a shadow fell over her. Evan was reaching into the basket of wet clothes. "Let me help," he said.

"Thank you," she said.

As he helped spread out the laundry, she took a moment to admire him. From the first day she'd met Evan she knew she liked him. He made her laugh with his corny jokes, but more than that, he was an excellent listener. She really appreciated that. They'd been together for so long, she really couldn't imagine being without him.

Evan was also attractive, even if Jill had snidely told her otherwise the night before. She rather liked his large nose, and the dark brown hair he couldn't seem to keep neat. It wasn't that he needed a haircut. His hair seemed to have a mind of its own, and stuck up in the front, no matter what he did.

Without even realizing she was doing it, Tara reached up and smoothed her hand over his hair.

"I suspect I could shave myself bald and it would still stick up," Evan joked, as she made the attempt.

Tara laughed herself. "Perhaps," she said, and then teased, "I'd like to see that."

He winked then, "Stick around long enough, maybe you will. The men on my side all start balding early. It's a curse. Unruly hair while you have it, and then none a short time later."

He made an overly dramatic gesture with his hands trying to hold down his hair and she laughed even harder. Evan wrapped his arms around her for a hug and crushed her to him.

Tara rested one hand on his chest. "We really shouldn't," she giggled.

"Brief handholding is acceptable for someone courting," Evan grinned. "As is a chaste kiss and occasional brief embrace. I looked it up. Is that...is that something you'd be willing to do? Court? The book says we can. With rules."

"What book?" Tara looked up at him in surprise. "Where at?"

Reluctantly, Evan stepped back to see her better. "Mark found a book they gave us with all kinds of rules and guidelines and wisdom about stuff back then. I guess now, actually. You know, this time period. Way back when. It's confusing. Anyway, I was looking over it."

"Well, then," Tara said happily. She stood on her tiptoes and gave him a light kiss on his lips. "That makes me feel better," she said. Her cheeks turned pink. "Maybe...maybe we can try. I'd like that. I've been waiting for a while for you to ask me, actually."

So, no more avoiding me?" Evan asked.

"I wasn't avoiding you," Tara answered, feeling hurt. "I'm trying to follow the rules." She bit her lip then. "I want to be honest. Fair. I signed a paper saying I would be. You know that's what we have to do if we want to win. A hundred thousand dollars each is a lot of money. Think what we could do with it."

Evan sighed and ran his hand through his hair. "I know," he said, unable to stop the grumble from coming out. "Just...I want us to be more official. I've been wanting to ask you for a while, if you'd like to be more than friends. It just never felt like the right time. Here, it finally did. But that has come with its own set of problems. Here, I can only look at you, not touch."

Tara laughed. "That's part of the charm of this era."

Evan reached for her hand. "When we leave, I look forward to it being with you as my girlfriend. I've been waiting a long time to call you that."

"I can't wait to tell Lindsay it's official," Tara said. "Let's read those courting rules together later. I'm so excited you spotted them. Perhaps we can figure out just what we're allowed to do when courting, without breaking any rules of the era."

"I'd like that," Evan grinned.

"I'm glad you said something," Tara said. "I was getting worried."

"Worried? About what?" Evan stared at her, his expression concerned.

"Well, it's just sometimes it's hard to know when you like something or have an opinion. It's like you don't always want to share." She grinned then, hoping to remove any sting from her words, "It's been like that as long as I've known you. I was getting a little worried you were sick of me."

Evan crossed his arms. "Never. I'd never be tired of you. But I like to process things. This is a new place and it's a lot of work. I've had a lot on my mind, and more time to think. Thinking makes me quiet. It's who I am. Got to accept it."

"I do," Tara said softly, worried now she'd upset him.

A movement from the corner of her eye caught her attention, and she turned her head. "Did you see that?" she asked with a frown.

"See what?" Evan asked.

"I thought I saw Jill staring at us."

"Let her stare," Evan shrugged. "She can have Mark if she wants him. I'm all yours." He moved in for a quick kiss, then pulled back as a nearby bush shook.

Tara jumped backward. "What's that?" she asked, her voice almost squeaking. "Who's there?"

There was nothing but silence. She and Evan stared for a long moment. Just when she thought she'd imagined the movement and noise, the bush shook again.

"Evan!" she shrieked. "Oh my gosh! What if it's a bear or something?"

He moved closer. "Don't worry," Evan said. "I'll keep you safe."

Tara felt better. Having him here meant a lot. Not just so that she could do this experience with him, but also because she trusted him completely, that he wouldn't let anything hurt her.

Picking up a large stick, Evan stalked over to the bush and swished the stick. Nothing happened. He tapped on the bush with the stick, and shook it slightly. The bush's branches swayed. Still nothing. Evan grinned at her, and Tara relaxed.

"Maybe a bird or rabbit?" she called.

"Probably," he said. "But I'll check it just to be sure. Well, if anything's there." He went around the backside, pushed aside a portion of the brush, and gave a shout.

Tara felt faint. What was happening? She wanted to rush forward, but her legs seemed to freeze. She couldn't tell from the strange yelp he'd made, and the grim expression on his face, if she should be worried and try to run for help, or to be worried and run for her life, hoping he was right behind her.

"E-Evan?" she asked. Her throat felt so tight it was difficult to get even the single word out. Her mouth opened and closed, but nothing more came out. It must be something horrible. Some grisly discovery.

Evan squatted down by the bush, or collapsed, or something. She couldn't tell. When he didn't stand back up, Tara did the only thing she could think to do. She screamed as loudly as she could.

CHAPTER 6

When Tara screamed, it startled Evan. His head snapped up, then back down at the tiny white kitten hiding in the brush. "Tara! Hush," he called. "You're scaring it."

Jill and Mark were running toward them, and screeched to a stop just as Tara stopped screaming.

"Scare what?" she asked.

Evan didn't answer, but instead reached into the bush, then pulled out the kitten. Both girls gasped and moved closer to him.

Mark asked, "Where did that come from?"

"Ohhh it's so tiny," Tara cooed, swooping in. She took it and nuzzled the kitten, who let out a soft mew.

"I wonder how this got out here," Mark said. "I mean, we're pretty alone. The little thing must have wandered pretty far."

"Or has a feral mother," Evan said.

"Who cares?" Tara said. "She's mine now. Look how skinny she is. Poor thing hasn't eaten for a while. I'm her mama now."

"Let's think of a name for it," Jill said, just as adoringly to the kitten as Tara felt. She stroked one of its tiny paws.

"Snowball," Tara said instantly. "That was the name of a kitten in a book I loved as a little girl. I think that's the perfect name," she proclaimed.

Mark walked over with a grin. "I'm sure glad it turned out to be a kitten, and not something dangerous. I heard that scream and thought it was a bear or something."

"Me too," Jill said. "It's a little wilder than I thought out here. Even though we haven't had trouble with animals like that, I know we have them."

"We do?" Tara asked, looking nervous.

"Yeah, the area has bears and foxes and racoons. You never know when one will be rabid." Jill shrugged. "Their claws are nothing to joke with. You'll get shredded in an instant."

"All the more reason it's good we rescued Snowball," Tara said, cuddling the kitten closely. "I'm going to put her in the cabin. Please, don't anyone let her get outside until she's used to things and can find her way back."

The others agreed, and Tara walked toward the cabin. Evan started to follow when Jill stopped him with a hand on his arm. He looked over at her.

Jill's eyes were wide and a flirtatious smile was on her lips as she looked up at him. "You were so brave back there," she said. "It could have been anything, and you rushed right into the danger."

Evan wasn't sure why, but he blushed a little. He didn't have a chance to answer, because Tara returned from the cabin. Her steps hesitated as she saw him with Jill, and her eyes landed on the other girl's hand.

"Always happy to do my part to help everyone," Evan said and then stepped away from Jill. "That's why we are all here, right? To do our part and win the prize."

Jill nodded and walked toward Tara. She turned back, with a wink and a whisper, and said, "Come see me later, if you want real fun, not the kind with rules attached."

Evan didn't know what to say. He felt a little shocked. He hadn't realized that Jill was interested in him. Honestly, he wasn't the least bit interested in her, so her comment was surprising.

Tara stepped up next to him. Her eyes flicked toward Jill and there was a hint of a frown on her face. "Ready for that walk?" she asked.

"Yes," he said, and took her hand in his. "Remember, hand holding is allowed."

"Can you remember anything else that falls in the courting category?" Tara asked. "I'd love to see that book. I bet there are all kinds of other interesting things in there too. I wonder who wrote it, and why we didn't see it sooner."

"When we get back, I'll grab it," Evan offered. "I want to look at it more too. I don't remember that much, really. I only gave it a quick look."

Tara didn't answer and they walked in silence for a moment a short distance away from the cabin. Evan thought he might be wrong, but there was a strange feeling he was getting from Tara. He wondered if it had something to do with Jill a little bit ago.

"You okay?" he asked. "You seem quiet."

"I'm just tired," Tara said. "Long days, lots of manual labor. Lots of time with your thoughts. Like you said."

"What thoughts are those?" Evan asked. "Us?"

Tara stopped at a mossy bed and settled herself. The cabin was still in sight, but they were far enough away they had privacy. "Us. My old life. My job. You. You know, I thought if I came here, maybe it would give me some time to figure out what I wanted from life. What I felt was missing."

Sitting next to her, Evan nodded. "I was hoping the same," he said. Then he nudged her. "I figured out part of it, anyway. About us." He grinned at her, but she wasn't looking. He asked, "Have you had a chance to think about your questions?"

"A little," Tara said, running a hand over the soft moss. "Honestly, at the end of the day I'm pretty tired, almost too tired to think, but one thing has really struck me."

"Yeah?"

"Yeah. That I'm so tired, but I'm not worrying, you know?" Tara looked into the distance and sighed. "Well, not about work, anyway."

"What do you mean?" Evan asked.

She was quiet for a moment, then answered, "Before, I'm not sure I ever went to bed without worrying. Did I finish everything I needed to do at work that day? Were my numbers high enough? What was I going to do about this account? How was I going to break it to this person that there was a quality issue? What new name could I call the beige color that's nearly identical to last year's beige color? You know, all those work questions."

"I do know," Evan said. He started ticking off on his fingers. "Can I get to the rest of those emails in the morning or do I need to answer them now, even though it's almost midnight? Is there a more efficient way to collect that data? How many cups of coffee will it take not to fall asleep from boredom tomorrow during the meeting and my analysis of the newest data report that's nearly identical to last month's?"

Tara laughed. He loved her laugh. It was so light, so tinkly. He wanted to make her do it again.

"You understand perfectly," she said. "But, have you worried about that stuff while you were here?"

"No," Evan answered, and then shook his head. "I've not. But I do worry what it's going to be like when I get back. If I can get caught up." He sighed then and rubbed a hand through his hair. "Who am I kidding? I'll never get caught up. I wasn't caught up before I left."

Tara's hand found his and she squeezed it. "I understand. It's just part of how it is, I guess."

"Does it have to be?" Evan asked. "Isn't there something better? Or at least something I can do that I enjoy?" He sighed. "I shouldn't complain. It pays well. It could be much worse. I just don't feel...happy there. You know? Makes me wonder what else there is. It makes me wonder if I should have even come."

"What do you mean?" Evan felt Tara tense. "I thought...I thought that you wanted to come with me."

"I did," Evan said. Frustration filled his voice then. "That's not what I meant. Of course I wanted to come. I wanted to be with you."

"But this," Tara waved her arm. "This place isn't really something you wanted."

"I'm not sure what I want," Evan said. "Other than you. That's rock solid." He squeezed her hand and nuzzled her head. She smelled wonderful, even out here, without her usual vanilla scented soap. "I just need time to figure it out. I wish I had answers to all my questions about the future."

"That's not something I can help with," Tara said. "But worrying about the future is sure something I wonder about too. Maybe that's why I enjoy the past so much. It seems simpler. Even though I'm here now, and it's not, it's really much harder at times, it still feels better. Relaxing." She laughed then and met his eyes. "Does that sound weird? I'm worn out, but...happy."

"Happy because you are here?" Evan asked.

"Yes. Happy I am here, with you," Tara said, shifting closer to him. "Thank you for coming with me. I wouldn't enjoy myself without you. I'm happy that I'm doing all of this stuff. I didn't realize I was capable of doing so much without modern conveniences. I make all the food from scratch. We grow the ingredients too. Isn't that amazing? I'm really proud of myself and it's a good feeling to know I can do these things. But what about you? Are you happy to be here? Even if maybe you aren't sure if you should have come?"

Evan leaned close. "Yes. I'm very happy to be here," he said. He hesitated, then brought his face to hers for their first real kiss ever. Their lips barely brushed when a loud clap of thunder shook the tree they were under.

"Oh no! Not more rain," Tara yelped as she startled, and she stood up.

Luckily, the cabins weren't far away, Evan felt glad they were within distance, and the two ran, making it to the clearing the buildings were in just as the first raindrops fell.

Tara raced to pull the laundry off of the line, and Evan helped her. The rain started to fall harder. "See you at dinner?" Tara called as she stood in her cabin doorway.

"You bet," Evan called from his. He went in and dropped his and Mark's clean laundry on their small table.

Mark looked up. He was scraping his pocketknife over a small piece of wood. "Good walk?" he asked.

"It was about to be good, then it started raining," Evan said. He sorted the clothes and dropped them on their pallets. "Hey, that book I was looking at earlier. The one with the rules and stuff. Know where it's at?"

"Sorry, no," Mark said. "I thought you had it."

"I left it on the table when we went to go for breakfast," Evan frowned. He spent a few minutes looking around, but it was gone. "Guess I'll ask the girls at dinner," he said, and walked over to the single window in the cabin.

He watched the rain for a moment. It was starting to lighten. Through his window, he could see into the girl's cabin. Tara was over at the stove, and Jill was at the table, looking down at something. She looked up and caught him staring at her. She smiled and blew him a kiss, just as Tara looked over.

Tara's eyes met his with a hurt expression, and she turned back to the stove, her stirring now frantic almost. Evan couldn't help but close his eyes for a moment. Great. Just great.

Evan opened his eyes and didn't miss the smirk Jill had on her face. He frowned and glanced at Mark, who shrugged. What was she up to? He was sure it was something, he just didn't know what.

CHAPTER 7

Tara didn't understand why she had seen Evan and Jill flirting. Hadn't he just told her that he was ready to be more serious about their future? Said the word courting? That meant just her, only her, with a possible ring in their future. It made her wonder what had changed. Or had he always been flirting with other people when she wasn't looking? The thought didn't feel right as soon as her brain processed it, but she didn't know.

She knew people can act one way for a long time, then act another without any reason other than that's just who they were. Had Evan ever acted that way before? Her mind thought back over the years. She couldn't remember a time where he had.

Her throat felt tight and her chest ached from the hurt. She shot a glance over at Jill, who was smirking and writing in her notebook. Her eyes narrowing, Tara felt determined to see what was in it. Was there something about her inside? Or something about Jill and Evan?

She quietly neared where Jill was sitting, but the other girl closed the book and slipped into a pocket. For some reason that really irritated her. "Why are you always writing in there and hiding it?" Tara asked, her arms crossed.

Jill gave her an innocent expression. "I'm journaling. That's what people do, isn't it? Even back then? Don't we know so much about the era from letters and journals? You know we are allowed to do that. You also know it's not polite to read someone's innermost thoughts and feelings."

Tara nearly sputtered as she answered. "I-I guess so."

How had Jill known so much about this time was from journals? She sure didn't seem to know much else about the time period, so that really surprised her. A thought came to her then. Maybe she'd read it in that book Evan had talked about.

"Hey, Evan said that he found a book about this time period. I wanted to look at it. Have you seen it yet?"

"No," Jill answered, shaking her head. "I haven't. The guys must have it."

"I guess," Tara said. She shot another glance at Jill. The notebook peeked out of her pocket. How could she get it for a moment to read what it said?

"Oh shoot," Jill said suddenly. "I left the pail of cream in the barn."

"The rain is lighter. You can grab it real quick," Tara said.

"Yeah, I better. We need to make butter before it spoils." Jill stood, but then tripped over the bench at the table. She hopped over to the door and left.

Tara turned to stir the vegetable stew she had cooking when she spotted something. The notebook Jill was always writing in! Hurriedly she picked it up, getting it hidden in her pocket just as the door opened and Jill came in.

"Be back in a few," Tara said.

She left, going to the one place she knew she'd be able to have total privacy—the outhouse.

The small building could have been more horrible, she supposed, but Tara really wasn't sure how. They'd been warned to keep their visits brief, watch for spiders both inside the outhouse and the hole waste dropped through, and assured it wasn't often snakes got inside.

Tara wasn't sure how people ever got used to such a thing, but she was glad that she wouldn't have to use this primitive toilet much longer.

Closing the door behind her, Tara latched it, reached into her pocket, and pulled out the small notebook. She took a moment to study it. It was small, about the size of the palm of her hand. The cover was Navy, and it was spiral bound at the top. She opened the cover and held her breath, unsure what she'd see.

Then she flipped to the next page, then the next. What was all this stuff? It wasn't a journal. There was nothing about her in here, or Evan. So, what was it?

In the dim light, Tara squinted as she turned the pages. In neat handwriting were simply notes. *Add more animals. Ramp up tension with exhaustion. More chores? Consider S2 with more couples. Couples=drama.*

Tara shook her head. Was Jill thinking up ways the show could continue? Why? She flipped through the rest of the notebook, only filled about halfway, then sighed. This wasn't what she'd expected, not one little bit. She thought it was going to talk about Evan, and Jill's burning desire for him. Maybe about how goody goody or annoying Tara was. How she didn't like Mark much. Not this...whatever this was.

Disappointed, Tara stuck the notebook in her pocket and left the outhouse. She was going to have to sneak it back to Jill somehow. Hopefully she hadn't noticed it missing.

When Tara went inside, Jill had a panicked look on her face and was pulling back the blankets on the bed.

"What's wrong?" Tara asked. "Did you see a spider? Oh, please say it wasn't a mouse."

"No, I just...lost something," Jill said. She moved to a box where she kept her belongings.

"What's missing?" Tara asked. "I'll help look."

"Nothing," Jill answered.

Tara shook her head and crossed her arms. "If it was nothing, you wouldn't be so upset."

"Fine. My journal," Jill said. "Happy?"

Tara ignored the snippy tone. "I'll help you look," she said. Then her eyes lit up. "You went to the barn to get the cream. Did you have it then?"

"Yes!" Jill gasped. "It must have fallen on the way."

They went outside and Jill hurried into the barn. Tara waited a moment until she couldn't see her, and dropped the notebook on the ground. Then she bent over and grabbed it, making sure to press it against the dirt to get a smudge on it. That would make it look more realistic.

"I found it!" Tara called.

The words were hardly out of her mouth when Jill rushed from the barn and snatched it out of Tara's hand. Without looking, she put it in her pocket. "Thanks," she said, and went back inside.

Phew. None the wiser.

Tara followed her inside, and stirred the stew. Once again she counted how many days were left. She couldn't wait.

"What's the first thing you're going to do when you leave?" Tara asked.

"Shower. And then eat pizza. And cookies I didn't have to make." Jill didn't even hesitate.

"Me too. And go out on a proper date with Evan. I want to see that book he found." She sat down heavily with a flop, then brightened as she noticed the rain had stopped. "I'm going to go see if I can borrow it."

A short walk and something different might be just what she needed to shake off that feeling that Jill was up to something strange.

"I'll go with you," Jill said.

Tara didn't answer, even though she wanted to tell Jill that she didn't want company. She had been hoping to get a little more time with just her and Evan. She wanted him to explain just what that was she'd seen between him and Jill a short while ago when they looked like they were flirting. Hopefully, it had been a misunderstanding. But she'd never know unless she asked.

And right now, she thought as she and Jill walked over to the guys' house, is that she had two choices. Ignore it for now, or ask in front of Jill and Mark. Neither were ideas that she liked. Being in this situation, around others all the time and bound by rules that dictated every aspect of their lives from what they wore and ate to when they had to do chores and what kind, was starting to get really old.

She had the feeling if Jill wasn't here, things would go a lot smoother. She seemed determined to make everything harder than it needed to be. But why? Was there some rule she missed about how if one person left, their prize money was split among the others?

Tara shot Jill a sideways glance then knocked on the guys' door.

Mark answered. "Hey."

"Hey," Tara said.

Evan joined Mark. "It's stopped raining," he said, as he looked in surprise at the sky. "Good. We were just about to start chores."

"Can I borrow that book you were talking about?" Tara asked.

Evan frowned. "I can't find it," he said. "I thought I'd read more, while it was raining, but I don't know where it's at. Mark didn't see it either. I was going to ask if one of you had it."

Tara filled with disappointment. "I don't," she said.

"Me either," Jill said. "Too bad. I wonder where it went. I guess you can't read about those courting rules now," she added, then clapped a hand over her mouth.

"Wait. I didn't say anything about that," Tara said, piercing Jill with her hardest stare. Jill's tone had sounded a little too smug for her liking.

Jill quickly answered, "No, but I heard Evan talk about it." She shot him a quick glance and fluttered her lashes. "But like I said, I don't need rules to court."

Tara took a sharp breath. Jill was flirting with Evan right in front of her? "What's wrong with you?" she asked. "Why are you doing this?"

"Doing what?" Jill asked.

"Everything!" Tara said, throwing her hands up. "Making everything difficult. You don't do your fair share of the chores, you go around spying on all of us and writing it down, you're flirting with Evan now, and doing it right in front of me!"

Mark stepped closer. "Let's calm down," he said.

"I'm calm," Jill said, with a smile. "It's Tara who seems a little—"

"Forget it," Tara interrupted. "Just forget it. It's obvious you've got something against me. Maybe you're trying to get rid of me because you think that will make you popular or you'll get my share of the prize. I don't know, but whatever it is, it won't work. I agreed to come and play by the rules, and that's what I'm going to do."

"So, does that mean without knowing the rules of the era about courting, you and Evan aren't going to date?" Jill asked, her voice sticky sweet.

Tara looked up at Evan. He wore a concerned look on his face. How had it happened so suddenly that everything had gone wrong in the last hour? The chance to court, by the rules, was also now gone, since the book was. It was obvious someone had taken it, and likely Jill. But why?

And more importantly, was that going to make Evan upset with her? Probably. She knew he didn't take this as seriously as her. She also knew that he was only here because of her.

"It's okay," Evan said, interrupting her spiraling thoughts. "We are playing by the rules, all of us. Anyway, this isn't a discussion for anyone other than me and Tara to be part of."

Tara gave him a grateful look. Evan stepped toward her and took her hand. "Don't worry," he said. "We will either figure it out, or we wait a little longer until we leave." He squeezed her hand. "I'm okay with either, as long as I'm with you."

Jill stepped forward, and said in a hurt voice, "But...Evan. What about you and me?"

Tara's jaw dropped. She looked between the two of them and dropped Evan's hand. "What about you two?" she asked.

"There's nothing between us," Evan said firmly.

When she scanned his face, Tara's first instinct was to believe him. After all, he hadn't even known Jill before they came. She just wasn't sure she wanted to ask any more questions. The answers might be ones she didn't want to know.

She couldn't help it though. Her voice wobbled, "If that's the case, then why do I keep sensing something going on?"

"You don't trust me?" Evan asked, his face filled with hurt. Then his eyes sought Jill, and his jaw clenched. "Why are you doing this?" His tone was angry while his eyes were locked on hers.

Jill opened her mouth, then closed it. She glanced at Mark with an uncertain look. Tara caught the little head shake between the two of them and narrowed her eyes. "You two are up to something," she said, pointing her finger accusingly.

"Yeah," Evan said. "What are you up to? Are you trying to force us to leave? Or force just one of us to leave?" He crossed his arms. "I really don't trust either of you. Jill, you are always sneaking around with that little book of yours. Mark, you do some weird stuff too. I thought I heard you talking to someone the other day. No one was there, but what I did make out, made you sound suspicious."

Neither of them answered. Tara took a deep breath. "Whatever. I'm done with you. Done with all of this. This was a bad idea. I'm stupid for thinking that I'd be able to enjoy myself here, spend time with my Evan and get to know him better, and have a simple, happy life for a month, leaving all the drama behind that the corporate lifestyle is filled with. Looks like I was wrong. There's drama here too, even though there didn't have to be."

She spun around and stalked to the cabin, ignoring Evan and Jill calling after her. She was done. There were four days left. All she had to do was get through, and she'd be back home away from all this mess.

CHAPTER 8

Evan yelled after Tara when she left, but she didn't turn around. He didn't blame her. Jill and Mark were looking off in the distance, at their shoes, anywhere but at him.

"I know we don't know each other well," he finally said, taking a deep breath, "but seriously, what are you doing? Why are you causing problems?"

When neither of them said anything, he added, "It's not like it's some cutthroat competition. You don't have anything to gain by us leaving. That's the part I really don't get."

When Jill and Mark glanced at each other again and then looked away, Evan scoffed, then walked toward the cabin where Tara was. He paused and said over his shoulder, "She's right. You two have taken something that could have been really great, and turned it into a stressful drama zone. I'll be glad if I never see you two again."

He knocked on the cabin door and opened it, surprised to see Tara with her face grimaced in pain and a cloth pressed to her leg. "Are you okay?" he asked.

"Something stung me," she said. "I don't know how. These skirts go nearly to the ground. My whole leg feels like it's on fire."

"Let me look," Evan said, and squatted on the floor. He moved aside her skirt.

"My ankle," Tara moaned.

"Tara, this isn't the time to be concerned about showing your ankles," Evan said, rolling his eyes. "Anyway, the cabin door is open. Propriety is intact. Your honor is safe."

"No," Tara said. "That's not what I meant."

Her voice sounded funny, and Evan looked at her. She was flushed and breathing heavily. Evan put a hand to her face. It was blazing. He jumped up. "Jill! Mark!" he yelled, then ran back to Tara. He picked her up and laid her on the bed, and looking at her bite mark, his whole body tensed.

This wasn't good. He didn't know what bit her, but something wasn't right. Her ankle was swelling. It was also starting to turn a strange darker color. He glanced over as Jill and Mark came in.

"What happened?" Jill asked.

"She's been stung or bitten or something. It's swelling really bad," Evan said.

"Do you see a stinger?" Mark asked and he pulled up his sleeves.

"No," Evan said. He pointed then. "But that's the puncture."

"I'll get cold water and a rag to put on her foot," Jill said, jumping up and disappearing.

"Single puncture, likely an insect. Perhaps a spider." Mark said.

Tara started shivering. "I'm so cold," she whispered.

Mark touched her head. "You're clammy. Evan, go get our blankets."

Evan didn't ask questions. Instinctively, he knew this was bad and Tara was in danger. Anything that was swelling this fast wasn't good. The problem was that they were out in the middle of nowhere. What if they couldn't take care of her? He ran to his and Mark's cabin and pulled the blankets off the bed, returning with them.

Jill was back, and had laid a cool cloth on Tara's ankle. Tara was restless, and nearly unconscious. "This isn't good," Jill whispered, and looked at Mark.

Evan folded the blankets and set them next to Tara, while Mark checked her pulse. "It's too fast," he said. "I wish I knew what bit her. It's so swollen, I can't tell. My instinct is a spider. We are in the woods and there aren't many flying things with stingers around here."

"She's very flushed," Jill said. "Her breathing doesn't seem right. I think she's having an allergic reaction."

"Be right back," Mark said.

"Where are you going?" Evan asked.

Mark hesitated, traded glances with Jill, and said, "Emergency first aid kit."

"We have an emergency first aid kit? Is it a modern one? Or some weird 1800s stuff?" Evan jumped up to follow him, but Jill shook her head. "Let him go alone," she said.

He wanted to argue, but something about Jill had changed. He couldn't quite put his finger on it, but she seemed...serious? More in charge? No, that wasn't it. He didn't have time to think about it now, but whatever it was, it was different. Almost like...it was who she really was. Not who she'd been for the last few weeks.

Jill took the rag off of Tara's ankle, rewet it and laid it back on. She also put one on Tara's forehead.

Mark came back with a large box. It looked like one of the crates in the barn that had always sat in the corner with some sacks nearby. Evan had never thought much about it, figuring it was some sort of set piece for the camera to catch and look all barn-like.

Evan watched as Mark set it on the floor and opened it. Inside, it was filled with first aid equipment. From modern day. Thank goodness.

"I've got things to bandage," he said, rifling through, "and a small knife if we need to drain the wound. I'm not sure either of those are the best thing right now. Here's some ointment." He continued to rummage through.

"What about epinephrine?" Jill asked, her voice calm. "Antihistamines? Those should be there as well. Look for a small pouch."

"Epinephrine?" Evan asked, his head darting between the two of them. "What are you talking about? And who are you really?"

Mark pulled out a small red case and dropped a blood pressure cuff and stethoscope next to it. "Yes, there are four EpiPens right here. I've also got prednisone and antihistamines. I'll administer the steroid and antihistamine first. I don't think she's in anaphylaxis, but I'll be ready."

Evan grabbed his arm. "Hold it. You aren't doing anything until you talk to me first," he said.

Calmly, Mark answered, "Evan, I'm a medic. I do this every day. Tara seems to have started with a mild allergic reaction, but it's growing past that. If it progresses, then we will need to treat her in order to make sure she recovers. The best way to do that is to treat her now and see if she responds, and if not, treat her aggressively with what we have until we can get help."

Mild? This was mild? Swallowing hard, Evan nodded and stepped back. Mark returned to Tara, and said, "Tara? Can you hear me? I need you to swallow this medicine."

Tara let out a whimper and parted her lips slightly.

"Give me some water," Mark ordered. Jill had it in his hand in a moment. He put the pills in her mouth and dribbled water in. Tara swallowed and whimpered again.

"It's okay," Jill said soothingly, holding Tara's hand. "We've got this. Mark knows just what to do, and help is on the way. You're going to be just fine."

Evan paced. Jill followed him. "What if she's not?" he whispered. "We're here without any help. Without any way to contact someone."

"That's not true," Jill said. "Remember, the cameras?" She gestured around the room. "Once Tara started having problems, the person watching the screens would have called for help."

"I don't know what's worse," Evan groaned. "Her being sick right now, or how she's going to act when she wakes up in a hospital, this close to winning."

He moved close to the bed. "I'm not leaving you," he promised Tara, and reached for her hand. "I'll make sure you are okay."

"She will be," Mark promised, a hand on his shoulder. "We've got medicines, and I'm sure help is on the way."

Evan didn't answer. He couldn't. Nothing made sense. How was it Mark and Jill were so calm?

He shot them a look. The two were talking quietly across the room. It almost looked like they were arguing about something.

"There you go again," Evan said, irritation thick in his voice. "Keeping secrets."

"Not in a bad way," Jill said. "I promise."

She looked honest, but it didn't matter. He still felt angry at her. "I'm sick of this," Evan said. "Why can't you just tell us what's going on?"

"I promise we will," Mark said. "As soon as Tara wakes up." He took a deep breath. "You're right. You deserve to know the truth."

CHAPTER 9

Tara shivered. It was so cold. No, it was hot. Wait. She was cold again. Her eyelids felt impossible to lift. There were voices, but they sounded so far away.

Her leg hurt. Her head hurt. She was thirsty. Tara tried to move her lips. Nothing happened. She was frozen, trapped inside of an unmoving body. What was happening?

A small sound must have escaped, because a person leaned close to her. Her eyelids cracked open, then fell heavily closed again. She didn't recognize the person. It wasn't Evan, or Mark, or Jill.

There was a sharp feeling and her eyelids raised enough to see a tiny white paw with claws digging into her arm. She smiled as Snowball cuddled in close to her. Had the kitten been there the whole time?

"Tara? How are you feeling?"

It was Evan! He was here. She wanted to tell him she was cold. And hot. And thirsty. But her lips wouldn't move. Wait. Yes, they did a little.

There was a funny croaking sound. What was it?

"Give her a drink," Jill said from somewhere. "She wants a drink."

Oh. That sound had been her? A cool liquid dribbled into her mouth. Tara had never tasted anything so good. It must be ambrosia. Did that mean she had died? But why was Jill there? Was there nowhere she could escape her?

Her thought was broken by Evan saying, "Drink slower. There's plenty of water, but not too much at a time."

Water? Water never tasted this good. He had to be wrong. This wasn't water. It was life.

Tara tried to open her eyes. They wouldn't budge, but with her parched tongue and throat feeling better she let out a deep sigh, and fell back asleep.

What a very strange dream she was having.

CHAPTER 10

Evan sat back, disappointed. "I thought she was waking up," he said.

"The medicines are making her groggy," the doctor said as he checked Tara's oxygen level with a small device that went on her finger. "She'll wake up soon and feel a lot better."

"I'm glad you came so quickly," Jill said. She handed out bowls of stew. "We almost made it without needing anyone from civilization. But this is going to be great for ratings."

Great for ratings? Why would Jill have said that? Evan glared at her. He wanted to say something, remind her about Tara in the bed nearly fighting for her life, but Mark's hand on his shoulder and small head shake made him swallow back what he'd wanted to stay.

Even looked at his bowl. He wasn't hungry, but he knew he needed to eat. There wasn't anything else to do to help Tara, and if he didn't eat, then he might not be able to help her when she needed him. At least, that's what Jill had told him the last few meals.

It was true. He was tired. Evan had been sitting here next to Tara for three days. What should have been a celebration today for their last night, was a watch to make sure Tara didn't worsen. So far she was stable, improving, in fact both the doctor and Mark said, but Evan was concerned that could change at any point. He'd hardly closed his eyes, and when he did, he made sure he was holding her hand, so if she moved, he'd wake up.

Evan raised the spoon to his lips, not even tasting the hearty white bean and chicken stew. He kept his focus on Tara.

Regret swam in him. He never even had time to reassure her after she'd gotten upset. To tell her how much he liked her. Loved her. That Jill wasn't someone he was interested in.

He closed his eyes for a moment and drew in a shuddering sigh. When he opened them again, he watched Tara. They'd had a whole month together. Yet, he felt like so much of it was wasted. Not because of the rules. He saw that now. With the courting rules, it actually made him get to know her, to want to be with her more.

No, the time wasted was because of the drama that kept arising. From Jill and Mark. He shot them a look. They'd still not told him their secret. When Tara woke up, they sure had some explaining to do.

The evening dragged on. Jill kept coffee and tea available, and even attempted baked apples with brown sugar and cinnamon that weren't too bad tasting, considering she wasn't much of a cook.

The doctor read a book, and Mark did the chores around the place. They all knew Evan wouldn't leave Tara's bedside, and no one even asked. The closest he came was when he started making Snowball a scratching post out of some old rope he wrapped around a short, skinny log and bolted to a larger, flat piece of wood. Even then, he was still at the bedside, just not touching her.

The kitten seemed to approve, and left her spot next to Tara only long enough to stretch on the post, lap some cream from a bowl, and use the litter box Mark had filled with wood shavings. Then she was right back, curled next to Tara's head.

It was getting late, and the doctor walked over. "Let me check her again," he said, peering down at Tara's ankle.

It had greatly improved with the needed medicine, but the doctor still checked on it, and her vital signs, every few hours.

"She looks much better than she did this morning," he said, sounding pleased. "And far better than when I first got here."

"I feel better," a faint voice said from the bed.

Evan's head shot over to Tara, and Jill and Mark rushed over. Tara was looking around the room. When her eyes met his, she smiled. "What happened?" she asked.

"You thought you'd spend the final days in bed, that's what," Evan teased.

When she started to move, he helped her to sit, arranging the pillows behind her back. Tara frowned at the doctor. "Who are you?"

"A doctor," Jill said, offering Tara a mug of tea.

"I'm going to check in with the studio," the doctor said, and quietly left.

Evan watched closely as Tara frowned. "I have questions I want answers to," she said.

"Same," Evan said.

"We'll tell you everything now," Mark promised.

"We? So you are in on all the weird stuff," Evan said, sitting back slightly.

"Sort of," Mark said.

Jill shrugged. "No sort of," she admitted. "We were in on it. But it's for a good reason," she said, holding up a hand to stall Evan's protest he had forming.

"We're listening," Tara said. She crossed her arms.

Jill and Mark exchanged that look Evan was really starting to hate. "Okay," Mark said. "Well, we work for the station."

"What?" Tara gasped.

"Yeah. The head producer is my dad. It's a long story, I'll tell you later, but basically, the only way I could actually work for the station and not get accused of nepotism was to take an intern spot, ace it, and then start moving up the ranks. Hello intern spot," she said, waving her arm around. "I hate the outdoors, so whoever thought I'd be perfect for this, well, I hope for their sake I never find out."

"What's your story?" Evan asked, glancing at Mark.

"I took the job because what I really want, is to audition for a role on the soap opera *Hour by Hour*. The chores have really buffed up my body," Mark added, flexing, "so I'm really hoping when we get back to get through the auditions and land that role."

"A soap opera?" Tara stared at him, and her jaw dropped.

"Not just any soap," Mark argued. "It's *Hour by Hour*. That show's been running for decades, and has churned out more actors and actresses who've gone on to be successful on shows and movies than any other show."

"If you say so," Evan said, his eyebrows raised.

"I'll also pay off my student loans for college," Mark said. He shrugged. "If I get the part, anyway. I've got a backup plan if I don't. Something medicine related."

"So, that's it? Jill flirted with Evan and didn't do chores, and Mark did it all to what...increase the drama and gain muscle?" Tara looked between the two, her face filled with disbelief.

Evan squeezed her hand. "I only love you," he said. "No one else."

Jill crinkled her nose. "Okay, when you say it that way, we kinda sound awful. I promise, we aren't. Anyway! There's something we've been just dying to tell you. Remember how the producer said there was an extra prize that could be won?" Jill asked. Her face was doing something funny now.

Watching closely, Evan could see she was getting excited and trying not to seem like it or smile. The result was a weird twitch. Did that mean for her it was good news, or for them? He narrowed his eyes. "What about it?" Evan asked, unable to wait any longer.

Mark grinned. "We just got told about it. It's a big one. Big, big prize. And we think you two will be perfect for it."

"Wanna spit it out already?" Tara asked.

Jill burst out, "What would you say if I told you that you two had the opportunity to live here for an entire year?"

Now it was Evan and Tara who traded looks. There was a flash of surprise, then one of disbelief that crossed over Tara's face.

"You are leaving something out," Tara finally said. "I sense it. Spit it out. All of it. Don't leave anything out."

Mark spoke now. "This place is about twenty-five acres. There's the barn, this cabin, and the smaller one. All the animals, the supplies, a wagon and horses. Everything here, lock, stock, and barrel is all yours for the keeping, free and clear, along with the hundred thousand dollars each, plus another hundred and fifty thousand each, if you can live here for a year like you are in the 1800s."

"A year?" Tara whispered.

Evan wished he knew what she was thinking. But he sure knew what he was thinking. A year? Would they have to live with Jill and Mark? What about his job? Tara's job?

"A year?" Tara whispered again.

Even looked over at her. Her eyes were wide.

"Yeah. The catch is just you two though. Mark and I aren't doing it. No way," Jill said.

"It would all be ours? Forever?" she asked. "A quarter million dollars each, plus the property, and everything on it? And you'll give us a wagon and horses?"

Jill nodded. "That's right. All yours. Your dream, Tara. To live like this. And after that year, you can do anything you want. You can put in plumbing. You can get electricity. You can do anything."

"You'd have an entire year to figure out what you want to have, and what you are happy with," Mark said.

"What about the cameras?" Tara asked.

"Only in the barn, the kitchen, public places like that," Jill assured her. "And that way, if there's another medical emergency, you can get help."

"Would we ever get to see anyone else?" Tara asked.

"Your family and friends can visit whenever they want, as long as they also follow the rules," Mark grinned. "So is that a yes from you, Tara? You want to have a chance to win?"

"Wait, wait, wait," Evan said. He couldn't believe Tara was asking these questions. Was she seriously considering it? "What about your job? Your family? The hard work here?"

"What about the fact I could live the life I've always wanted to and have an incredible financial future for my family one day?" Tara asked. "Do you know how long and how hard I'd have to work to save up to buy a place like this, and the two hundred and fifty grand on top? How many mind-numbing hours I'd need to spend? Rent isn't cheap, neither is what I pay to commute to work each week."

"I hadn't thought of that," Evan said. "That's a lot of hours looking at data sheets." He grimaced. "A lot of hours."

"And meetings," Tara told him. "Endless meetings and clients and pressure to meet deadlines."

"I see why this is appealing," Evan admitted. "I hate those meetings. And those data sheets. Are you thinking it's a yes, then?"

"I would love to do it," Tara said. "I know you might not want to. And I know it isn't fair of me to ask you to stay if you don't want to."

"I want to think about it," Evan said slowly. "There's a lot then I'd have to do. That evil cow won't milk herself," he added. The others laughed and he shrugged. Apologetically, he said, "I'm not sure really if just the two of us could manage this place. And what if you needed me and I'm all the way in the other house asleep? I need to think this through. Do what's best. We were going to plan a future together, remember? A little hard to do that if we're on camera for a year."

He glanced at Tara as he said what he was thinking, and she nodded, but he didn't miss the flash of sadness in her eyes.

"Of course," she said, quickly. "I understand completely."

There was an idea forming in his head. Something had struck him. This was it. The answer to all his questions. His problems at work, the feeling of stress and never catching up that was waiting at a desk back in the real world. The schedules for him and Tara that never quite matched up so they could be together.

"The problem," Evan said slowly, as though he didn't hear her, "is that if I stay, it can't be like it is right now."

"What do you mean?" Jill asked. She frowned. "You'd need to live here like it's the 1800s."

"Yes," Evan said. "That part I get." He turned to Tara. There was a tightness in his stomach where his nerves all sat in a lump. "What I meant is that I can't stay here for an entire year and see you and not be able to hold your hand or kiss you or hold you," Evan explained. He gave a soft laugh as he shook his head. "I had no idea how hard it would be to be here and not be with you."

Tara bit her lip. She nodded. "You are right. We'd have to stay away from each other, wouldn't we?" Her shoulders slumped. "That would be part of following the rules, wouldn't it?"

Mark nodded. "Yes. Unless you—"

"It's good, man. I've got this part," Evan said, winking at him.

Tara blinked at him, looking confused. "What?"

"Unless I did this," Evan asked.

There was a loud gasp from Jill as he dropped onto a knee and took Tara's hand. "Will you marry me? And we will spend the next year living like crazy people in the middle of nowhere with no running water or electricity and loving every minute of it?"

"Yes!" Tara squealed and wrapped her arms around him tightly. "Oh, my gosh! I always wanted an 1800s wedding gown!"

Everyone laughed, and Evan leaned over and gave Tara a kiss. Jill cleared her throat and he backed up. "Better make that dress quickly," he teased.

"I'll start tomorrow," Tara grinned.

EPILOGUE

Tara held a hand up to her eyes, blocking the sun. Sunglasses were one of the first things she'd be getting. Right after indoor plumbing. Winter in Pennsylvania was rough when someone needed water or the outhouse. The no electricity thing wasn't too bad, but that was on the list too. She was debating even trying solar.

Evan came out of the barn, two buckets in hand. He handed her the smaller of the two. "Fresh cream," he said.

"Good, I want to have a nice supply of butter for when Mom and Dad and Lindsay come visit," Tara said.

"I can't believe this place is about to be ours," Evan said, his voice filled with wonder as he looked around.

Tara let her eyes follow his. There were the buildings, of course, but what she loved most was the small forest with the tall trees and cool moss, the tall waving wheat off in the distance, and the small dots of flowers that were both wild and planted from seeds Jill had given her and Tara planted on what she called her "prairie."

"We are going to have quite the celebration," Tara agreed. She rested a hand on her stomach. "And it's good that I get to give birth in a real hospital in a few months. I love this time period, but I love my modern conveniences just a little bit more."

Evan nodded. "You said it. Can't wait for that plumbing. Hauling water was okay at first, now it stinks."

"It's made your muscles huge," Tara said, as she ran her hand down his arm.

They walked back to the house with the pails and Tara dumped the cream into the butter churner. Evan sniffed appreciatively. "Is that a pie I'm smelling?"

"Yep," Tara said. "From the berries we picked the other day. I figured we need to celebrate!"

"You've done an incredible job cooking on this thing," Evan said with a head shake as he looked at the old stove.

Tara had to agree. It was true. She almost liked cooking on it. It was easy to set something on the top to simmer and if she had to go do something, she didn't need to worry about it boiling over or burning, especially if she hadn't stoked the fire.

"Let's eat," Tara said, and dished out the food. It was a hearty meal of a thick ham and potato stew with fresh spring peas, cornbread, and tea. After dinner, Tara cleaned up and Evan worked on sharpening some of his tools.

It was getting late, but neither made ready for bed, even when they started yawning. Just as her eyes were getting heavy, there was the sound of a car driving down the road. Tara's face lit up, and she brought the pie to the table, along with four plates and four forks.

Evan opened the door, and Jill and Mark rushed in. "You did it!" Jill squealed as she hugged Tara. "A whole year!"

"We'll get the cameras out of here first thing tomorrow," Mark promised, "just as soon as you do your exit interviews. Have you thought about what you are going to do now?"

"Not really," Evan said. "We've talked about if we wanted to go back to work or just try to live off the prize money for a while. I think first thing, adding some electricity—"

"And plumbing," Tara interrupted.

"And plumbing," Evan agreed, "and just see what happens. It's been nice not worrying about the rat race for a while. Maybe I'll do some freelance work. I'm not in a hurry to ever get back into data analysis."

"Maybe I'll write about this experience. Make a series of books," Tara smiled. "I'm ready to leave design behind. It didn't fulfill me the way this has." Then she gave a content sigh. "I can't believe it. It's ours. It's all ours."

Evan wrapped his arms around her. "I can't think of anything better in life happening. I've got you, we've got this place, a kiddo on the way, and two good friends."

Jill and Mark grinned at him. Evan raised a brow. "You two are standing awfully close together," he said, gesturing between Jill and Mark. "Anything we should know about?"

Her cheeks red, Jill said, "Mark and I have been dating for a while now. He asked me to marry him, and I said yes."

Tara squealed, then squealed even louder as Jill added, "I hope you'll both be in the wedding party."

"We wouldn't miss it for anything," Tara promised. "After all, if it hadn't been for you two, we might not be married."

"Oh, you didn't need us for that," Jill said, shaking her head. "You two are perfect together. That's why we tried so hard to shake things up for the ratings. I'm glad it didn't work. You deserve each other." Then she giggled, "And you two sure had enough mishaps on your own without us, you didn't need us to do that at all."

"Sure haven't missed that cow," Mark chuckled, and slapped Evan on his back. "You sure looked funny when she kicked the bucket up and it landed on your head."

"Or when the roof fell in over the kitchen, and a raccoon started running around the house, Snowball chasing after it," Jill laughed.

Mark slapped his knee, "Oh! What about when the outhouse door flew open when—"

"We get it, we get it," Evan said, interrupting Mark. He rolled his eyes. "Glad that we were such good material."

"You sure were. In fact, the test viewers love you so much, we've decided to add a season to the show, and rename it." Jill rubbed her hands together.

"To what?" Tara asked, as she cut into the pie.

"*The 1800s Experiment*," Mark answered, helping himself to the first piece.

"Sounds pretty interesting," Evan said. "We sure did have to experiment a lot to figure things out."

"We're casting for next season," Mark said. "So if you know anyone, let us know. You'll have neighbors!"

"Neighbors," Tara mused. "You know, if we got enough of them, we could build up our own little town."

"Nuh uh," Evan said.

"You could be mayor," Tara continued.

"I'm not listening," Evan said, putting his hands over his ears. "We've done this once. I want indoor plumbing!"

"Plumbing...maybe we call the town Plumb—"

"Nooo!" Evan groaned. He glared at Jill and Mark. "See what you've started?"

Jill just smiled. "Season three ideas," she said, and whipped out her small notepad.

The friends laughed, ate their pie, and enjoyed each other's company. Tara couldn't remember the last time she'd felt so happy and so full. She knew what she wanted in life, everything felt right, and Evan felt the same.

As she settled into bed in the wee hours of the morning, when her eyes closed and she started to drift to sleep, she could almost hear the *Little House on the Prairie* theme song. Instead of Ma and Pa though, it was her and Evan, standing proudly looking at their house. In her arms was a little girl.

Smiling, she turned to her side and let the darkness wash over her. Home on her very own homestead. There was no better place to be.

WANT THE OTHER SIDE OF THE STORY? FIND JILL AND MARK ON AMAZON!

Jill works hard to prove she's more than just the daughter of the TV station's head producer. She's also tired of fetching donuts and delivering file folders. So, when an opportunity arises for her to apply as an assistant in casting? She's more than ready. There's a catch though. She's got to earn the interview by stirring up trouble on a new reality TV show. How hard can that be?

Also desperate for a better spot at the TV studio, Mark longs to hang up his medic bag and step into the spotlight as an actor for a popular soap opera. He's been promised a free pass through the first round of auditions if he does the boss a favor. In the slow days of the 1800s, there will be plenty of time for him to learn his lines and practice his smoldering gaze. It's going to be a piece of cake.

Except Jill didn't expect it to be so difficult to cause trouble, and Mark starts rethinking his future life as a star. Add in some complicated romantic feelings that arise, the stress and guilt of stirring up trouble, and Jill and Mark can't wait to get out of the 1800s—and an experiment gone wrong!

https://www.amazon.com/Jill-Mark-1800s-Experiment-Sarah-ebook/dp/B0CVV8GWXY

Chapter 1

Tara didn't even bother to hide her scowl as she balanced two coffee cups in one hand and a box of pastries in the other. The morning had been rough and she doubted it would get any better. She'd spilled the first two cups on her new sweater and had to turn back to the bakery to replace them. Then her skirt had gotten caught in the elevator and torn, and at least a dozen people had laughed at her.

"Here you are," she said, setting the bakery order gingerly on the Your Television Favorites producer's desk.

YTF was a major cable network, and an incredibly popular one. For the last year, she'd been an intern there, doing everything from fetching coffee and dropping off papers from one office to the next, to picking up people from the airport one moment, and lunch orders the next. No two days were the same, which was good.

Sometimes.

The days were always long and she was tired when she went home, but there was always that hope of moving up in the company, and that's what kept her going.

Today had been pretty mundane. Going out to the bakery had been the highlight of her day. Which sounded pretty bad, when she thought about it and her sweater. Thank goodness she had a change of clothes at the office. As she'd changed, she reminded herself she wouldn't be stuck as an intern forever. She was sure of that.

The most interesting thing she'd gotten to do so far in this job was when they were casting for different shows and an extra body was needed here or there to hold a light, spritz on hairspray, or act as an off camera person to feed lines to. She enjoyed that, and liked watching both the screen tests and going over the forms that potential contestants filled out when the opportunity was granted her.

"Thanks, hon," the producer said, taking a sip from his to-go cup and sitting back in his chair. "Sit."

Jill sat, brushing her dark hair out of her face. She didn't like the feeling she was getting. It was radiating in waves that made her feel nervous. It was a little bit "you are in trouble" and "I've got something to tell you." She didn't like either. But especially coming from him. That made it worse. She'd been in that meeting last week when he'd fired three people right after his first sip of coffee.

"Want one?" the producer, Clark Masterson, offered the pastry box.

Jill leaned forward. "Thanks, Dad."

He cleared his throat. "I'm not Dad during the work day," he reminded her.

"Right. Sorry." Jill bit into the cherry Danish and tried to ignore the heat in her cheeks.

Working at YTF was a little bit of a blessing and a curse. With her dad the top producer, at first, many people thought she'd be getting special treatment and good jobs. Luckily for them, though not for her, that couldn't be further from the truth.

Her first month there, she'd been in janitorial. She'd emptied trash cans, scrubbed toilets, vacuumed, and picked up so many gum wrappers that she never wanted to see another stick of Juicy Fruit again. She hadn't complained, though. She knew better. If she did, she might not get to move up for a very long time—if he didn't fire her first.

Thankfully, an intern spot had opened after just a few weeks and she was given it. That's when she moved into fetching. On a slow day, she logged fifteen thousand steps, if that said anything.

But, so far, she'd managed to not step on toes, make a few friends, but most importantly, prove to others that she wasn't there because of who her dad was, but because she'd earned the spot.

And she had. Every day, she worked her hardest. Jill had her eye on a position, and she was going to keep going until she got it.

Her dad set his croissant down and gave a slight frown. That made her worry. Whatever he was going to say couldn't be good. The bite of cherry Danish slid to her stomach and landed like a lump. She reached for her spiced cider to wash it down.

"There's an opportunity. If you want it," he told her.

"What kind?" Jill asked. She'd learned to ask for specifics. After being a yes woman the first few weeks, she'd been taken advantage of, and didn't want to go down that route again. There had been a few unpleasant "opportunities" passed her way. Never again, if she could help it.

"For a show," her father said. He pushed a thick file over to her.

Jill took it, and opened the cover. "*The 1800s Experiment,*" she read, then skimmed over the premise. "Huh. A guy, a girl, and the stressors of historical living for four weeks. Will they fall in love or will they become mortal enemies. Sounds a bit...dramatic," Jill said, looking up.

"That's our business," her father shrugged. "So, you interested?"

"In what way?" Jill took another bite.

"We need two more people there to make it look like the stakes are higher," he answered.

Jill tilted her head. "I don't understand. Why not make it a group then? Get eight or ten people?"

"Viewers are tired of that," her father answered, pushing another paper toward her and tapping his finger on a bar graph. "With endless reality shows for dating or survival, it's gotten a little tiring. This is different. It's one couple—well, two—and living like in the past. We've even found the perfect girl," he said, handing her an application.

"Tara James. Favorite show," Jill read. "*Little House on the Prairie*. Greatest wish, to live like I was in the 1800s." She looked up and laughed. "It's like she was made for this."

"She sort of was," her father agreed. "We were originally casting for *The Moving Maze* or *So You Think You Could be a Doctor,* but when we pitched the idea, our test audiences weren't interested. This one, they were."

"So, who would you pair her up with, if the goal is to see if they fall in love or not?" Jill glanced down at the application again. "You'd want it to be someone she'd have a shot with, not a random stranger, if they're just going to be there four weeks. That's really not a lot of time."

"That's the good part," her father grinned. "She filled out an application with her best friend. Who left some pretty heavy hints that he likes her."

"Let me see. This could be good." Jill snatched the paper her father held out. "Evan Adams. Favorite thing to do. Doesn't matter, as long as I'm with Tara. Favorite thing to eat. Anything Tara makes." She looked up. "You've found your couple alright. Who is the fourth person going to be?"

"I'm not sure yet," her father admitted. "I'm still thinking about it. Are you interested?"

"Maybe," Jill said. "But where would I come into play? If this is to be about them?"

"We don't want this to be too perfect," her father said. "They're going to have a chance at a huge cash prize and, if ratings are high enough, an even larger one. But we don't want it to be too easy. It can't all be sunsets and smiles, and happy music playing in the background. There's no viewership or sponsors with that."

"Soooooo, I'm to...?

"Shake things up a little. Do your part to help, but stay alert. If things are going too well, put a little drama in. Flirt with the guy. I don't know. Viewers aren't going to know you are a plant until the final interviews."

"It sounds a little weird you telling me to flirt," Jill said, raising a brow. She crossed her arms. "What do I get out of this? As an employee of YTF, I wouldn't be eligible for a prize."

"Not a cash one," her father agreed. He gave her a long look. A strange fluttering formed in Jill's stomach, and she leaned forward, holding her breath. Here it was. The reason for the strange feeling coming from him.

"There's an opening coming up for an assistant to the casting director," he told her. "It could be yours."

Jill leaned forward, smacked her hands on the desk, then stood up and tucked her dark hair behind her ears. "Well then, you've got yourself a shaker," she said. "They'd better watch out."

"Perfect," her father said. "I knew I could count on you. I'll send the where and when to your email once I have all the details. Now," he said, patting the thick file, "I need you to get this over to Jenkin's office. Tell him to contact the contestants right away."

Taking the thick stack of files with a nod, Jill hurried out. She could hardly believe it. A chance to be a casting assistant. It was a step in the right direction. An opportunity, indeed.

Excitement filled every inch of her. It wasn't until she'd shut the door behind her she realized there was a problem. A big, big problem.

NOTE FROM AUTHOR

Thank you for taking the time to read The 1800s
Experiment, Tara and Evan!
Could I ask for one small favor? Reviews like yours on
Amazon mean so much to me and help others to find my
books! Even just a single line means a lot!
Want a FREE book?
Stop by my website to get your no strings attached **FREE
book**. It's my gift to you, as a thank you for reading this
book.
www.sarahlambbooks.com

ABOUT THE AUTHOR

Sarah Lamb is the mother of two boys and wife to a teacher. She spends her days writing historical romance in the beautiful Shenandoah Valley.

WANT MORE OF SARAH'S BOOKS?

Find them all on Amazon!

https://www.amazon.com/stores/Sarah-Lamb/auth or/B098H3SGLK